John W. Marsh, Allen Gardiner, Waite H Stirling

The Story of Commander Allen Gardiner, R.N.

with sketches of missionary work in South America.

John W. Marsh, Allen Gardiner, Waite H Stirling

The Story of Commander Allen Gardiner, R.N.
with sketches of missionary work in South America.

ISBN/EAN: 9783337314132

Printed in Europe, USA, Canada, Australia, Japan

Cover: Foto ©Andreas Hilbeck / pixelio.de

More available books at **www.hansebooks.com**

THE STORY

OF

COMMANDER ALLEN GARDINER, R.N.,

WITH

SKETCHES OF MISSIONARY WORK IN SOUTH AMERICA.

BY

JOHN W. MARSH, M.A.,
VICAR OF BLEASBY, NOTTINGHAMSHIRE.

AND

WAITE H. STIRLING, B.A.,
SUPERINTENDENT MISSIONARY FOR TIERRA DEL FUEGO.

Fourth Edition.

LONDON:
JAMES NISBET & CO., 21 BERNERS STREET.
MDCCLXXVII.

PREFACE.

THE original Memoir of Captain Gardiner was published in 1857, when the Fuegian Mission had recently been established by the adoption of the plan recommended in memoranda, which were written by Captain Gardiner, in Tierra del Fuego, a little before his death. The missionary schooner, *Allen Gardiner*, had been built, Keppel Island had been selected for the station on the Falklands, and a clergyman had been appointed to superintend the working of the Mission.

Ten years have now elapsed since that time, and some account of the intervening period has been repeatedly asked for by those who are interested in the South American Mission. Hence, the present volume. Captain Gardiner's missionary researches in South America have been again related, and a short narrative has been given of efforts made for ten years to follow up the work in that great country. It will be seen that the early history of the Mission is in harmony with the suggestions and plans of the founder.

The following are some of the suggestions made by
him a short time before his death in 1851:—

I. NAME OF THE SOCIETY.

" Considering the wide field, which it is proposed that
the Society should enter upon and occupy, as far as they
have ability, it would be advisable to alter its present
designation to one more comprehensive and applicable,
viz.—The South American Missionary Society."

II. CLASSIFICATION OF THE SOCIETY'S OBJECTS.

" That the Society's operations be classed under two
departments, viz.—The Island, and the Continental."

III. PLAN FOR THE ISLAND OR FUEGIAN MISSION.

" To transfer the station to East Falkland, maintaining
there a few of the natives from Picton Island, for the
purpose of enabling the missionaries to acquire their
language. They should first be taught English, which will
enable them to become more efficient instructors in their
own language, and save much time, as they are exceedingly quick in imitating sounds, and repeating foreign
words correctly.

" The Government should be applied to for a tract of
land suitable for the Mission premises, and also sufficiently large for garden ground and pasture.

" During the progress of their education, and acquiring and teaching language, the natives should be employed in tilling small plots of garden ground, and also in tending stock on the Mission grazing farm.

" As soon as the missionaries have acquired the Fuegian tongue with sufficient fluency, it would be advisable to relinquish the station on East Falkland, and return to Banner Cove, which appears to be the most eligible spot for the head-quarters of the mission.

" Whenever it is deemed right that they should return to Picton Island, a suitable vessel should be purchased, fitted up expressly for that service, and sent out from England with stores and provisions, to convey them to their destination. This vessel should be regarded as the Mission House, and might remain so occupied as long as she could float. A brigantine of 100 tons would be the most suitable, and, if well built, would last for twenty or thirty years."

IV. SUGGESTIONS FOR THE CONTINENTAL WORK.

First—As to the Indian Tribes.—Having arrived at the Indian frontier, " the missionary, if he be prudent, and would not mar his future prospects, must be content for a while to pause. " To endeavour, without a competent knowledge of the native language, to gain their confidence and to locate within their borders, would be futile. It has been attempted by the writer in various points, and by dearly-bought experience, he is obliged to recommend a far different course; slower, indeed, but effectual, and the only one practicable. It is simply this, first, to acquire the language, and then, and not till then, to cross the Indian frontier, not indeed with the expectation of remaining among them, but as the first of a series of brief, oft-repeated visits, which, being judiciously conducted, will assuredly lead to the desired end—a permanent station in their country."

Secondly—As to the Spanish population.—" The Indian and the Spaniard being placed as they are in such close proximity, and in many instances with irregularly defined boundaries, the Society, whose main object is the instruction of the Indians, would materially further its operations by bestowing some portion of its care upon the Spanish speaking population also, for it is scarcely possible that any permanent good should be effected in one of these communities without producing a corresponding effect upon the other.

" Since the separation of the South American Republics from the mother country, education has been generally encouraged, and gradually extending among the laity, and a spirit of liberty is gaining ground. Instances could be mentioned when the efforts of the writer to distribute Bibles and tracts having been impeded by the ecclesiastics, the aid of the civil authorities turned the scale in his favour."

Thirdly—As to the English population.—In his last letter to his son, Captain Gardiner suggested to him employment in South America, both ministerial and missionary, in the following order:—

1. The Chilidugu Mission.

2. Our own fellow-countrymen in the Buenos Ayrean provinces, and in the Banda Oriental.

3. The distribution of Bibles and tracts.

Such were the enlarged views of Captain Gardiner, after a careful review of his past efforts. The last words were written as he felt the approach of death.

There are now three stations for missionary effort among the Indians—

Keppel, for Tierra del Fuego.

El Carmen, for Patagonia.

Lota, for Araucania, (called by Captain Gardiner the Chilidugu Mission.)

The Buenos Ayrean and the Chilian governments are favourable to the work of the South American Mission.

Missionary chaplaincies for the benefit of our own countrymen have been established at Panama, Callao in Peru, the Chincha Islands, where the guano vessels assemble in such numbers; Coquimbo in Chili, and Paysandù in Uruguay.

The promoters of the Mission are thankful for the progress which has been made. They are not discouraged because the work is slow, believing that the healthy growth of a mission is no more to be hurried than the healthy growth of a tree. While these pages are issuing from the press, the *Allen Gardiner* is returning to her work in the Antarctic Ocean. The four natives of Tierra del Fuego, who have been in England since August 1865, are on board. On the eve of her sailing from the port of

Bristol, Bishop Anderson, accompanied by other friends of the Mission, both lay and clerical, visited the little vessel, and held a farewell service on board.

God speed the *Allen Gardiner!* Be this our prayer! May she be a messenger of peace and life to men long sitting in darkness and in the shadow of death.

PREFACE TO THE THIRD EDITION.

THE issue of a third edition of this volume presents an opportunity for acknowledging the hand of God in the past events of the South American Mission.

The *Allen Gardiner* has seen twenty years of service since she first sailed, in the year 1854, on her sacred mission. She has carried the first missionaries to their home in the Falklands, and on pioneer voyages to Tierra del Fuego. She has brought Fuegians to the Falkland Mission Station and to England, and has again carried them back to be messengers of peace to their countrymen. She has had her perils, from collision at sea, from the intricate navigation of the Fuegian archipelago in stormy seasons; and on one occasion an attempt was made by fierce savages to set her on fire; but, by the blessing of God, she has been preserved through all these dangers, and is still employed in the same work.

Keppel Island was our first missionary settlement. Thither natives were brought for instruction, but this was only a temporary expedient, and now it has proved a stepping-stone to a station in the heart of Tierra del Fuego. Many of the natives have thankfully accepted the gospel of Jesus Christ, and thirty-seven of them have been baptized. For this great success we give thanks to God.

The details of this work are partly related in the
sixth and seventh chapters of· this volume, and the
rest in a little book, recently published, and entitled,
" First Fruits of the South American Mission."

The establishment of chaplaincies for English
communities in South America was effected on a
definite plan only ten years ago, as shewn in the
last chapter of this book, a chapter which has been
re-written for the present edition. As a movement,
therefore, it is too recent to be tested by its results.
The difficulties have been too many to be enumerated
here, but a few may be mentioned. There is, in the
first place, the permanent difficulty of providing
efficiently both for ministerial and educational work,
in a country or mining district, without exhausting
the chaplain's health or energy on the one hand, and
on the other without crippling the resources of those
among whom he labours, liable as they are in some
places to sudden fluctuations of trade. There is also
the difficulty of language, for he who takes the office of
chaplain to an English community in South America
should be perfectly acquainted with the language
generally spoken in the neighbourhood, whether it be
Spanish, Portuguese, or German. Still, although so
short a time has elapsed, we have to record with
thankfulness the establishment of five chaplaincies on
the East and five on the West Coast. Now, although
these chaplaincies are at considerable distances from
each other, yet the appointment of a Bishop of the
Falklands, whose licence all the Society's chaplains
are required to hold, has had the effect of welding
the separate links into one chain.

We have referred to the year 1854 as the date of the foundation of the Mission, and to the year 1864 as that in which the chaplaincy work on a large scale was inaugurated.

The year 1874 marks the commencement of the Amazon Mission. Mr Clough had previously ascended the Amazon for considerably more than 2000 miles, and had fixed on Santarem as a suitable basis for the work. Santarem is situated at the confluence of the river Tapajoz with the main stream of the Amazon, about 500 miles from Para. The journal, which Mr Clough wrote during the preliminary expedition, is being published monthly in the *South American Magazine.* In September last, accompanied by Mr Resyek of the Southern Mission in Tierra del Fuego, Mr Clough sailed for Santarem. Our readers must bear in mind that the Amazon Mission is a gigantic enterprise, and that, being undertaken, it must be prosecuted with vigour. Instead of two missionaries fifty are required. The Amazon is the highroad to a new Indian world, into which the gospel has not yet penetrated. We trust that every Englishman in South America will help the enterprise. We trust that every member of the South American Mission, at home and abroad, will work for it, and pray for a blessing on it. We ask of Him, " who had compassion on the multitude," to stir the hearts of all Christian people to come forward and give efficient help. J. W. M.

January 1874.

Ramirez

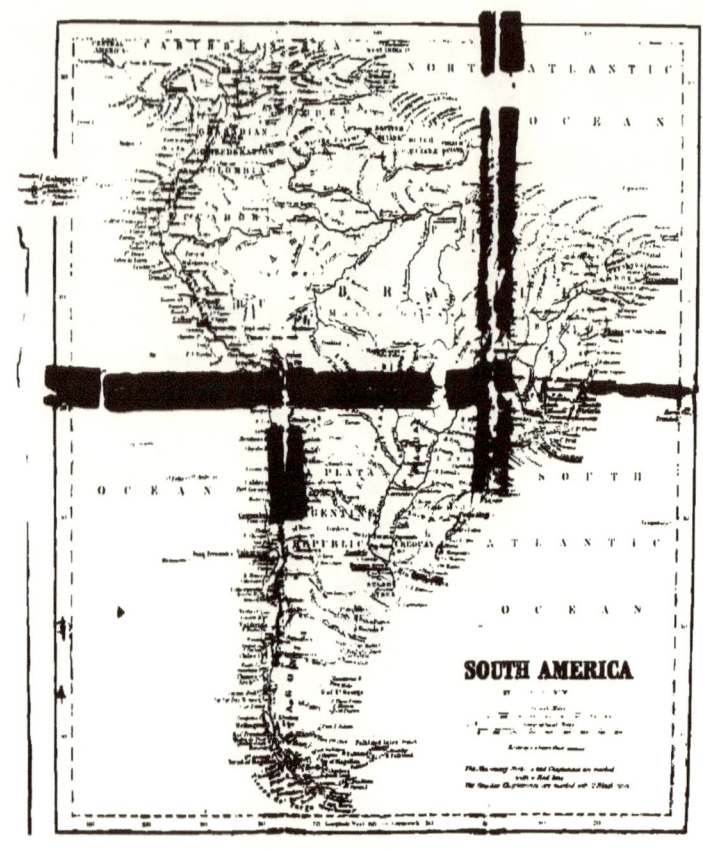

SOUTH AMERICA

CONTENTS.

MAPS.

THE STORY

OF

COMMANDER ALLEN GARDINER, R.N.

CHAPTER I.

ALLEN FRANCIS GARDINER.

ALLEN FRANCIS GARDINER was the fifth son of Samuel Gardiner, Esq., of Coombe Lodge, in the county of Oxford. He was born on the 28th of June 1794, at Basildon, Berks, where his parents were residing, while building Coombe Lodge.

There are few traditions of his boyhood left to us, but it is known that he was carefully trained in the principles of religion, and in after-life he was deeply sensible of the blessing afforded him in having God-fearing parents. He very early chose the navy as his profession, and, while a mere child, exercised his ingenuity in drawing plans for cutting the French fleet out of Rochelle harbour. He copied a small vocabulary out of Mungo Park's Travels, which he imagined might be turned to account in view of future explorations, and

A

on one occasion was found asleep on the floor, when he ought to have been in bed, giving as his reason when aroused, that it was his intention to travel all over the world, and that he therefore wished to accustom himself to hardships . all which incidents, though trifling, show how decided was the bent of his mind for travel and adventure.

He entered the Naval College at Portsmouth on the 13th of February 1808, and remained there two years, during which time he received much kindness from the Commissioner of the Dockyard, Sir George Grey, and from Lady Grey, whom he regarded throughout life as a second mother. Her letters and advice at a later period were of much use to him.

He first went to sea as a volunteer in the *Fortuné*, Captain Vansittart, on the 20th of June 1810, at Plymouth, and removed to the *Phœbe*, Captain Hillyar, at the Isle of France, in March of the following year. He served in this ship as midshipman till August 1814, when, having distinguished himself in the action between the *Phœbe* and the *Essex*, off Valparaiso, he was one of the officers selected to be put in charge of the prize, and was sent home in the *Essex*, as acting lieutenant.

In 1815 we find him serving as lieutenant in the *Ganymede*, then cruising in the Channel; and in 1819 he joined the *Leander*, carrying the flag of Rear-Admiral Sir Henry Blackwood, and sailed to the Cape of Good Hope, and thence to Trincomalee. The following year he exchanged into the *Dauntless*, Captain the Hon. Valentyn Gardner, and sailed to Madras, Penang, Malacca, Singapore, Manilla, and Macao. Here some of the merchants having applied to the admiral to allow a ship of war to fetch a cargo of specie from the Pacific, the *Dauntless* was detached for that service, and returned to Trincomalee. There she was refitted, and her captain having retired in ill-health, Captain Gambier took the command, and sailed to Port Jackson, and thence to Chili and Peru. Returning to China, they touched at the Marquesas and at Tahiti. On arriving at Sydney, Allen Gardiner invalided from the ship, and took passage to the Cape of Good Hope ; from whence, after a short delay, he sailed to England, and landed at Portsmouth on the 31st of October 1822.

His sketch-books and journals give ample and interesting accounts of his rambles and adventures in the various countries above enumerated, for he was always able to obtain leave of absence for some excursion, and his pen was equally ready for description or for sketching.

His connexion with the *Dauntless* marks a memorable era in his life, for it includes the time in which he steadily set his face toward the service of God; and in which he began to take that deep interest in favour of the aborigines of South America, and especially of Chili, which never afterwards left him. It was on this voyage, moreover, that he made his first acquaintance with missionaries, and had an opportunity of acquainting himself with the effect of their labours at Singapore, and again at Tahiti.

From this time we have, in addition to the journals before mentioned, a series of sacred meditations, written at intervals, chiefly on Sundays, and extending over a period of nearly thirty years. A few extracts shall be given, but only so far as is deemed necessary to illustrate the character, and show the actuating motives of a man whose conduct was before the world :—

"*Cape Town, August* 1822.—The last time I visited this colony, I was walking in the broad way, and hastening by rapid strides to the brink of eternal ruin. Blessed be His name who loved us, and gave Himself for us ; a great change has been wrought in my heart, and I am now enabled to derive pleasure and satisfaction in hearing and reading the Word of God, and in attending the means of grace. I trust that this alteration has, indeed, been effected by the Spirit of

God; yet I would not pause a moment to draw the contrast, except to give praise and gratitude to its merciful Author, lest I should be drawn into the fatal snare of presumptuous self-confidence; but, adoring my God for His goodness in not having consigned my soul long ago to the terrors of His indignation, I would carefully examine my heart as to the sincerity of its professions, and humbly implore at the throne of grace pardon for all that is past, and assistance to guide and strengthen me for the time to come."

"*At Sea, September* 1822.—If Christians are in the main more culpable than Jews, how much must they have to answer for who have, like Timothy, been taught the Holy Scriptures from their childhood, and yet have despised their contents? Such are the aggravated sins which, if unpardoned, must weigh my guilty soul to the lowest hell. What return shall I make to the Lord for so early, so unmerited a display of His goodness. Alas, how slow, how reluctant have I been to admit the heavenly Guest, who stood knocking without! Nor had He ever been admitted, had He not Himself prepared the way. And how is He now entertained? Too frequently am I ashamed to acknowledge the Hand that was stretched out for my relief, to own the Word that warned me on the brink of ruin, or to be seen supplicating that assistance by which alone I can be prevented from stumbling over the dreadful abyss. Is this religion? Is this love to God? Is such my usual conduct when warned of any temporal danger?"

About this time he had seriously in mind to change his profession, and had some communication with the Bishop of Gloucester on the subject of taking holy orders, but his ultimate decision was founded on the words of St Paul, "Let every man wherein he is called therein abide with God."

On July 1, 1823, he was married to Julia Susanna, daughter of John Reade, Esq., of Ipsden House, Oxfordshire, and in the following year was again called to active service in his profession, as second lieutenant to H.M.S. *Jupiter* in January 1824, and a few months later sailed for Newfoundland. On May 30, 1825, he was put in charge of H.M.B. *Clinker*, and remained in command of that vessel till he received orders to bring her to England, when he obtained his promotion as commander, September 13, 1826 ; but though he retained his early fondness for the service, and often applied for employment, he was never after this period actively engaged in it.

Captain and Mrs Gardiner lived successively at Maidenhead, Clifton, Southsea, Reading, and at Swanmore House, near Droxford, removing from place to place as his roving disposition and her delicate health gave occasion. Five children were given them, two of whom survive their parents. Wherever they went, the welfare of the poor was an object of interest to them both, and their memory is still dear to many persons. The various religious societies found an advocate in Captain Gardiner, and he once or twice accompanied his brother-in-law, the Rev. T. Woodrooffe, Canon of Winchester, in a tour for the Church Missionary Society. At length, Mrs Gardiner's increasing illness induced them in the year 1833 to remove to the Isle of Wight, in the hope of arresting consumption ; but she gradually declined, and died full of hope and peace on May 23, 1834,—a day the anniversary of which was devoted by her husband to fasting and humiliation to the end of his life. He writes :—

" *Ramsgate, June 29, 1834.*—Within the last twelve months the Lord in His wisdom has seen fit to take from me a beloved child and a tender and affectionate wife. My earthly comforts have been removed, and I pass my days in sorrow. Blessed be God ! He remembers that we are but dust. In my deep affliction, He has not left

me without mercy and great sources of comfort. The chief
of these is drawn from a review of the manifold grace
and love which He vouchsafed to my dearest wife, making her last days the brightest and happiest of her life.
Oh, what assurance of pardon, what joy, and peace, and
heavenly tranquillity, and ardent desire to be with her
Saviour, did He infuse into her soul! He has prepared her
for the enjoyment of His love, and is now filling her happy
spirit with all the fulness of His grace and glory. Tasting,
as I do, that the Lord is gracious, and feeling somewhat of
His redeeming love to my soul, my spirit exults in her bless-
edness. It is only my earthly affections that weep, and
would call her back. Such hope have I likewise, blessed be
the Lord our Righteousness, in the departure of my dear
child, who is now, I doubt not, with her sainted parent. I
sorrow not as those who have no hope, but have every encouragement to make my calling and election sure, that I like
them may enter into rest."

From this time he devoted himself afresh to the service of
God, and with all the force of his strong character, set himself upon a new course. As a work into which he might
throw his whole energy, and might hope, under the divine
blessing, to be of some use in the world, he chose that of a
missionary pioneer. With this view he went to Africa, and
explored the Zulu country, and started the first missionary
station at Port Natal. A few years later, he devoted many
months to an attempt to obtain entrance into New Guinea.
He went from island to island of the Indian Archipelago, and
from governor to magistrate, and from magistrate to governor, but all his efforts were baffled. Our limits will not
allow us to follow him into any of these countries, but we
shall proceed to trace out his various explorations in the continent of South America, and to record the triumph of faith
on the shore of Tierra del Fuego, prefacing the narrative with

the following solemn words of self-dedication and prayer, at the beginning of his missionary work :—

"*Barque Wellington, at Sea, Nov.* 11, 1834.—We are now, by the good hand of our God upon us, within one day's sail of our destination ; and as it is my earnest desire to take nothing in hand without seeking the aid and guidance of the Holy Spirit, I purpose to set this day solemnly apart for fasting and prayer, in the full expectation that the Lord will graciously attend to my cry, and make my path clear before me.

" O most holy and merciful Lord God, I beseech Thee to prepare my heart now for solemn prayer. Make me to feel abased in Thy sight for all my sins and provocations against Thee. No longer would I regard myself as my own, but bought with a price. Lord, make me cheerfully to give up all, and to follow Thee. Thou, Lord, hast put it into my heart to devote myself to the service of the heathen : oh that, if it be Thy will, I may be a humble instrument in Thy hand for good to their souls ! But I am as unequal as I am unworthy to do Thee any service. I know, O Lord, that without Thee I can do nothing that is pleasing in Thy sight, but at the same time, I thankfully believe that with Thee all things are possible. As a little child, I would therefore come to Thee. Lord, undertake for me, prepare my way, incline the hearts of Thy people to further my errand. Show me clearly the path of duty. Lord, if it be not Thy will that I should go to the heathen, permit me not to deceive myself ; but if otherwise, oh be Thou my Light, my Way, my Refuge. Direct me, O Lord, what I should do, to whom I should apply, and where I should go. If it is not from Thee, I desire not to go one step further. And I would plead before Thee Thy gracious promise, ' Come unto Me, all ye that are weary and are heavy laden, and I will give you rest.' Lord, I am laden with pride and selfishness. This is the sin which

(Thou knowest) doth most easily beset me. It is my burden.
Save me from its galling yoke, and bring me wholly to sub-
mit myself cheerfully to Thy yoke, which is indeed easy.
Having put my hand to the plough, may   back !
May Thy strength be made perfect in my

Having devoted his time and fortune   s and
more to the cause of the gospel at Port   n the
Zulu country, he left South Africa on   ut of
war between the Zulus and the emigra   t in
doing so, it was his opinion that there   aries
enough in the field to carry on the wor   the
restoration of peace should make it possible

His mind naturally reverted to the India   pas
and of Chili, whose heroic maintenance of   dependence had, years before, excited his a   ile
their continued Paganism was in his view a s   ch
to the supineness of the Christian world.

Captain Gardiner married again in the mo   er
1836. His second wife was the eldest daugh   v.
Edward Garrard Marsh, then of Hampstead,   s
vicar of Aylesford, Kent. For the next six y
his children were the companions of his wanderi
he frequently left them for a time in some fro
while he extended his researches alone into the
the country. This kind of life involved, of co
privations, but no one would pity the travellers
have witnessed the happiness that was experienc
and waggon, the merry play that went on in p
palanquin, the health that was secured in th
voyages, or the thankfulness that was nurtured
failing mercy and goodness which shielded them
danger.

CHAPTER II.

CHILI is a long narrow strip of picturesque and beautiful country, between the Cordillera and the Pacific, extending from the 25th to the 43d degree of south latitude. This great difference of latitude occasions a remarkable difference of climate. The northern provinces are hot and dry, being almost destitute of rain; but their mineral wealth is very great. In the southern provinces of Valdivia and Chiloe the rain pours in torrents for ten months in the year. The central provinces, from Valparaiso to Valdivia, enjoy a delicious climate, while the country is watered by countless rivers which run from the Cordillera to the Pacific. It is very fertile, and abounds in orchards, and produces large crops of grain. But the country, throughout its whole extent, suffers periodically from earthquakes.

The aboriginal tribes have been for the most part subdued, and are now mixed with their conquerors; but the warlike Araucanian tribes who inhabit the country which lies between the Biobio at Concepcion and the Calle-calle or Valdivia, still in great measure maintain their independence.

This was the people among whom Captain Gardiner made his first missionary researches in South America. He left Table Bay in South Africa on the 15th of May 1838, and conducted his family to Rio Janeiro, thence to Buenos Ayres, and across the Pampas to Mendoza. As soon as the season sufficiently advanced, they crossed the Cordillera into ᴊhili.

Arrived within sight of the river Biobio, he writes, in Dec. 1838 :—

" Being now within a short distance of what is generally reported as the territory of the Araucanian Indians, it was with much interest that we viewed the beautiful wooded hills on the opposite side of the Biobio ; and in the hope that it might not be long before we were located among them, I hastened to make the necessary preparations for a journey of inspection, in order to acquire that information for our guidance which could not otherwise be obtained.

" Had the Biobio been the real frontier, as I had been led to suppose, between this part of Chili and the independent Indians, a few hours would have been sufficient for my first journey; but such is not the case. From time to time, either by capture or purchase, a considerable tract of country on the left bank of the river, in which are some of the best farms and grazing grounds, has come to be occupied and claimed by Chilians. In proportion to the distance from the coast, the width of this acquired territory is diminished, until the Biobio itself becomes the actual boundary. I resolved to make my way by the nearest route to Los Angeles, the principal military post on this frontier, and thence to cross into the Indian territory at the most convenient point.

" At Los Angeles I waited on the commandant of the frontier, Major Barga, who, on receiving the passport which I had brought from the Intendente at Concepcion, kindly promised to furnish me with a letter to the officer commanding at the advanced post of San Carlos. . . . . From the conversation which I afterwards had with Captain Sinega, the commandant at San Carlos, it appeared that the nearest independent native chief of any note resided at a place called Piligen; and as this was not above twenty-four miles distant, it was agreed that I should set out at once, accompanied by the government interpreter.

"But there was an impediment to the speedy accomplishment of this plan. The Biobio, still a respectable stream, and in this part exceedingly rapid, had to be crossed, and the raft, by which alone it was fordable, was adrift, and a new one had to be prepared. It consisted merely of four trunks of trees about eighteen feet long, closely lashed together by hide-thongs to two transverse poles, one at each extremity, and when laden with ourselves and our saddles, it was scarcely an inch, in the highest part, above the surface of the water. As a matter of precaution, I not only took off my shoes and stockings, but also my coat and waistcoat, a measure which seemed to be regarded by the rest of the party as by no means unnecessary; for I had scarcely stepped upon the yielding raft when an inquiry was made whether I could swim or not. But the real novelty was the method of navigation. One of my horses, which was noted as an excellent swimmer, had not escaped observation by the way, and his powers were now to be tried in a most ludicrous manner. His tail was first smoothed out, and, the hair being doubled back, was firmly knotted to the end of the tow-rope: a naked lad then prang upon his back, and in plunged the horse and his rider. By a simultaneous effort of those on the shore, the raft he was destined to tow was at the same instant pushed off into er. Partly by swimming, partly by riding, now on one v on the other of the horse, firmly grasping through-ck of long hair always left for this purpose, the boy ed, by the aid of his heels, his hand, and his voice, in on the snorting and half-affrighted animal until he ed us to the opposite bank, where he was immediately ged, and the raft secured by the rope until we landed. lf-past two we were again mounted, and in three hours eached Piligen, crossing in our way the rivers Burau and Mulchaya.) The first person whom we met was Corbalan himself, the chief of this district, who was galloping his horse in another direction, but on perceiving us, cut across, and escorted us to his house.

"These people, who are excellent horsemen, always appear to best advantage when mounted. Corbalan was attired in a dark-coloured poncho, and seated with bare legs upon a rude kind of saddle-tree, above and beneath which a couple of sheep-skins were strapped, his great toes alone being thrust into the tiny wooden stirrups. A red band tied back from the forehead his long black hair, which flowed loosely on his shoulders, and concealed more than half his face, the expression of which was remarkably mild and intelligent.

"He received me with much hospitality; and before even a hint was given of any intended present, a sheep was ordered to be killed and dressed for our supper. The house, which is of an oval form, about thirty-five feet long, with a high pitched roof, supported by a row of interior p   ed but one apartment. The wattled sides, which   ut five feet high, as also the roof, which projected   ly over them, were neatly thatched with grass. Th   s of mud; there were no windows, but the door wa nient height and width. No excavation is made f place, which is always in the centre, where all the performed; but notwithstanding this, little inconv experienced from the smoke, which passes through ings left for the purpose in the roof, at each ext a high ridge-coping. Much cleanliness was observ preparation of their food; the meat was washed and upon a bamboo, by which it was held slantingly ove until it was thoroughly grilled. It was then pres us in wooden bowls. They had no milk, but gave usual beverage of parched meal and water, togeth

some piñones, the seed of the Cordillera pine, which is nu-
tritious, and in flavour resembles a roasted chestnut.

" Before we retired to rest, for which purpose Corbalan
ordered a smooth bullock s hide to be spread for me on the
floor, much conversation took place around the fire ; for besides his two wives, and other members of his family, some
men from the neighbourhood had joined the party. They
appeared to speak with great volubility, but the tone and
manner of the address—now a rapid and monotonous intona-
tion, now a single word, dwelt upon with a lengthened drawl,
and immediately succeeded by as rapid a sentence—had a
very ludicrous effect.

" During this conversation, some little progress appeared to
have been made towards the accomplishment of my object in
visiting this tribe. Corbalan was informed of my desire to
acquire his language, in order that I might impart to his
people the knowledge or the true God, as also of my wish
to obtain his consent to oring my family, and reside in his
immediate neighbourhood. Such a purpose seemed to be
altogether strange to his ear; still he made no objection, and
after a little further explanation, he seemed to enter cordially
into it. On being asked whether he should like to see the
Book in which God had taught us respecting Himself and
the way to heaven, he said yes, that it was good, and he
should be glad.

" An order had been given overnight to the neighbouring
chiefs to assemble as many of their people as were on the
spot, in order to welcome my arrival, and as soon as we were
mounted in the morning, Corbalan led us to the group, which
were collected under the tree at a short distance from his
house. As we approached, they mounted their horses, and
advanced towards us. Some few were on foot, but all in
their turn came up and took our hands. Corbalan apologised
for the smallness of the party, which amounted to forty-

five men, saying that the greater part of his people were absent in the mountains, collecting piñones. Among these,
however, were five inferior chiefs, two of whom in passing
presented me with a boiled fowl, which till then had been
concealed under their ponchos. Where to bestow this unexpected token of friendship in my case was rather puzzling;
the interpreter, however, at once relieved me of my dilemma
by depositing them in his saddle-bags. A small present of
indigo, beads, buttons, and handkerchiefs was distributed
among the chiefs—indigo, in particular, being much valued by
them for dyeing their home-spun wool.

"We then took our leave, Corbalan having previously agreed
to show me some of the inhabited spots in the neighbourhood, as I was anxious to obtain some idea of the amount of
population in this district, as also to select a spot for my
future residence. In every direction the country was beautiful, but without possessing any bold or romantic features,
excepting now and then, from some of the highest points, a
distant peep of the snowy Cordillera. But the grass was
rich, the surface undulating, and the trees in clumps and
groves were so ornamentally scattered, and discovered through
their openings so many park-like vistas, that I felt myself no
longer a stranger, the whole scenery being so similar to many
parts of England, that it was only when I recognised the
flowing ponchos and long, streaming hair of my companions,
that the illusion was broken. Two clusters of houses, in all,
not exceeding ten or eleven, were visited in this ride, all
apparently as neat, though not quite as large, as that of the
chief. Around all were little patches of cultivation, consisting chiefly of barley, wheat, and beans. On our return, I
selected a spot within a short distance of the chief's residence;
but I had no sooner pointed it out to him, than it became
evident his mind on this point had undergone a considerable
change; nor did he long disguise his sentiments, but plainly

acknowledged that, notwithstanding what he had before said, he must withdraw his consent. The reason which he assigned for this unexpected refusal was in all probability the result of a conference with the chiefs this morning, and appeared sufficiently weighty. Although still desirous that I should remain, he said it would not be safe: the Huilliches, his neighbours, a large and warlike tribe, would be offended; they would not permit a foreigner to live so near them; as soon as they heard it, they would attack him, and he should not be able to resist them. The result would be that both himself and his tribe, which could not muster more than a hundred fighting men, would be destroyed. I therefore took my leave of Corbalan, and soon lost sight of a spot which I shall ever remember with deep interest, and not without an earnest desire that the time may not be far distant when the dayspring from on high may visit this people, and the scattered hamlets of those secluded woodlands shall resound with grateful songs for redeeming love.

"My subsequent journey to Concepcion, where I arrived on the evening of the 13th, was a most unpleasant one, on account of the rain, which continued with little intermission throughout; and the roads, never good, had become so slippery, that it was with the greatest difficulty the horses could be kept upon their legs."

We pass over, for brevity's sake, a journey which was made to Arauco, near which Mr A. W. Gardiner now lives, a subsequent voyage to Valdivia, and the passage up the river Calle-calle to Quinchilca, and proceed to the narrative of a visit to the Indians on the Lake Ranco. There was some difficulty in procuring an interpreter; at length a man was found, and Captain Gardiner writes:—

"With this man, whose name was Pacheco, I set out on the 22d of February, and obtained shelter for the night at an Indian cottage. Within the short space of about two hours after leaving Quinchilca, the river Calle-calle is crossed no less than six times. The right bank exhibits in some places walls of gravel, large fragments having been detached by the late earthquake, carrying with them entire trees, many of which have taken root below, while others are still growing upon the projections which obstructed their further descent. Our route lay through a forest of bamboo. The stems, which are of a bright glossy yellow colour, and from two to three inches in diameter, are not tuberous, but solid, and so extremely hard, though light and elastic, that the Indians make use of them almost exclusively for their spears. So impervious a jungle is formed by these trees, that until a passage is cut, it is impossible to penetrate even on foot ; and when riding, much caution is necessary, to avoid the sharp points of the broken stem, which often impede the narrow path. When once entered, the effect is striking—a wall of yellow leafless stems, inclining as they rise, until they unite in a sharp angle overhead, like the cloistered aisles of some Gothic building.

"We continued our route early in the morning, until we reached a cluster of houses, among which was that of the chief,—whence I hastened forward to the brow of a rising ground, in order to enjoy a full view of the lake, of which I had only hitherto caught detached glimpses.

"An extensive sheet of water lay before us, probably about fifty miles in circumference. To the southward, by which its waters are conveyed to the Pacific, the land is comparatively low, and bare of trees, but to the northward it is hemmed in with bold ridges of wooded mountains, while the majestic Cordillera, clothed with snow, appeared to skirt its eastern limit. Eight islands, of different sizes, (some mere rocks,) appeared in the centre; one of them, which gives name to the lake, is inhabited, and about two miles in length. From the same spot, the scattered houses of Vutronway, (the name

of this Indian village,) with their several patches of cultivation, although half embosomed in apple groves, were visible.
Every object which met the eye seemed to speak its great
Creator's praise; but he for whose enjoyment all these beauties
were arranged had not yet learned to raise one song of thanksgiving to Him, who crowneth the year with His goodness!
In the earnest hope that it might please the Lord to permit
us to enter upon some work for His glory in this place, I
entered into a conditional agreement with a native to let his
house to me, until a more suitable one could be erected.
Then, as Neggiman, the chief, had gone on a visit to Arique,
I returned the same day to Quinchilca, and on the following
day, the 24th, set out for Arique. On my way thither I met
Neggiman, and from his lofty bearing at once recognised him
as the chief I was in search of. As he could only speak a
few words of Spanish, and I was alone, we all paused a while,
and the wood was made to echo with shouts and whistling,
until one of the party who was behind galloped up, and performed the office of interpreter. My object in wishing to
reside at Vutronway was then plainly stated to him, to which
he made no objection; but on hearing of my recent visit to
his village, he expressed some surprise that I should have
gone unaccompanied by any person deputed by Don Francisco Abierto, the commissary. After some further conversation, he said that, although he had never permitted a
stranger to reside among his people, still he would not withhold his consent, provided I made him a present, which he
specified, (one pound of indigo and a bar of salt,) and came
accompanied by a messenger from the commissary, with an
assurance of his concurrence in the arrangement. Thankful
for this apparent success, I proceeded to Arique, where the
commissary resided, and obtained from him a promise that a
guide should be in readiness to accompany me from Quinchilca the following Monday."

B

The next interview with Neggiman was at Vutronway.

" My new abode being cleaned out, I occupied it for the night, and early on the next morning, the 30th, the pack-horses arrived, and all were busily occupied in unlading and bringing in the baggage. I had just arranged everything, when Neggiman, followed by one attendant, was observed slowly approaching the house.

" Although it was a drizzling rain, he took his seat out-side, and inquired how long I thought of remaining at Vut-ronway. As no limit had been hinted at before, and I was unwilling to name one, I replied that I could not say—that it might be twelve moons, or two or three times that period, as I wished to become acquainted with his people, and to learn their language. It was evident from his manner that he had begun to waver in his determination, and he shortly informed me that he should limit my stay to one moon. Imagining that some lurking suspicion of my ulterior inten-tion might have prompted this sudden curtailment of his previous sanction, I gave him plainly to understand that I had not the slightest wish to purchase land, that I should always be prepared to leave whenever he saw fit, but at the same time that it would not be worth my while to bring up my family, with the understanding that on the following moon we were to return. He then again adverted to his determination not to permit Spaniards to reside among his people, adding that I was, moreover, a stranger from another country, and that he must therefore withhold his con-sent.

" Finding at length that his determination could not be shaken, I again felt the necessity of altogether abandoning what I could not regard as a legitimate opening, and of en-deavouring to approach the independent Indians from an-other quarter. Nothing now remained but to repack the furniture, a charge which I consigned to the arriero and the

interpreter ; and dejected, I own, but not in despair, I retraced my steps to Quinchilca."

The next journey was from Antilque to Cruces, and
from Cruces to Queule. It was fatiguing and "tedious,
not so much on account of the irregularity of the ground,
and the number of fallen trees. and logs, as from the thick
jungle of bamboo which overhung the path. At length
we entered a retired valley, skirted by the sea, into which the
river Queule was running. The neat cottages of the Indians,
scattered without order, the patches of barley, potatoes, &c.,
which now appeared, the windings of the river, and the distant roar of the surf, at once broke the monotony, and gave
a new interest to the scene. A native from one of the nearest houses conducted us to that of the chief, who soon made
his appearance, having just been bathing in the river. Two
low wooden stools, over which some skins were spread, were
brought by the women, and on one of these the chief, Wykepang, seated himself, after the customary greeting. He was
an elderly man, rather short in stature, of a stout muscular
frame, with coarse features, and of a somewhat blunt address.
His first inquiries were as to whence I came, and where I
was going, and he quite laughed at my design of going forward to visit some of the chiefs beyond. 'No Spaniards,' he
said, 'were living in those parts ; they were not permitted to
remain.' By the help of a native who understood Spanish,
I endeavoured to obtain his sentiments regarding the particular object which I had in view, inquiring whether he had
ever heard of God's Book. He expressed his surprise that I
should possess it, but seemed quite indifferent as to its contents. Being asked if he would permit a missionary, who
would instruct him and his people in that Book, to remain
with him, he quickly replied that he did not want one. I
proposed that he should allow me to visit him again, and
remain with him a sufficient time to acquire their language

To this proposition he seemed quite averse, and informed me that I must return, that he would permit me to stay one night, but that it would not be safe to remain longer, as the other chiefs would be angry, and make war upon him, if he allowed me to go farther. Our supper consisted of cold peas and hot potatoes. A skin was spread on the floor for my bed; and though much disappointed at the feeble prospect of gaining admittance among these suspicious people, I was enabled to sleep soundly, with my saddle for my pillow.

"Unwilling to take my leave without making one further effort, I again inquired what reception he would give me, supposing, on my next visit, it should be found that I had acquired his language. 'Then,' he said, 'you may come without fear;' and although he would not guarantee an equally favourable treatment from the chiefs who resided in the interior, yet from his manner, and the probability which he expressed of their relaxing from their usual restraints upon strangers under such circumstances, I felt that this was (humanly speaking) the hinge and turning-point of the whole matter in question. Taking my leave of Wykepang, we retraced our steps by the same tangled and tedious passes to Cruces, and arrived at Quinchilca the following day."

A few words of explanation shall now be given, to account in some degree for the difficulties which beset Captain Gardiner's every effort to settle among the Indians of Chili.

Throughout the whole tract of country, from Concepcion to Valdivia, a chain of forts had formerly tended to keep the natives in check, and in every fort Romish missionaries were stationed. There were at one time twenty-five of these stations; but the Indians eyed them with jealousy, and hated the soldier without loving the priest. The War of Independence, which began in 1810, relaxed the discipline of the frontier, and left the Indians in some degree their own

masters. Tucapel and other forts were taken and dis·
mantled by the Indians, and certain monasteries destroyed.
After the establishment of the republic of Chili, a new
policy was adopted. Friendly relations were established with
many of the frontier chiefs; the rank and pay of a major
was given to some, annual presents were made to others, and
commissaries were stationed, to reside with the friendly chiefs.
Thus those frontier tribes, whose chiefs were not above receiving Chilian pay, formed a barrier between Chili and the
more remote and more powerful tribes.

Two attempts were made by Captain Gardiner, in the
year 1841, to communicate with certain Indian tribes residing near the Cordillera. He relates the account as follows :—

"*Chiloe, July* 31, 1841.—To cross the Cordillera, in order
to communicate with the natives residing on the eastern side,
has been my object ever since our return to Valparaiso.
With this view, a journey to Talca was made, in the hope of
reaching the Pehuenche tribe by way of the Planchon Pass.
The result was unsatisfactory. Interpreters could not be procured in that neighbourhood—the location of the tribe was
not even known, and it was supposed to have removed for
some years back considerably to the southward. We accordingly came here, having understood that there was no lack
of Indians on the opposite side of the Cordillera, fronting
Osorno and Chiloe. My information, as far as it could be
available, was complete, and I had made all the preliminary
arrangements, purposing, if it were the Lord's will, on the
1st of September to have crossed to the opposite coast, and
by one of the most practicable passes which could be found,
to have struck directly eastward, until some traces of the
Indians were found. Since 1745 no one has crossed the Cordillera in this part of Chili, and as the route then taken was

much more northerly than that I should have attempted, considering the natural obstacles which were there encountered, we should necessarily have had to work our way by compass. But I will now explain why the execution of this plan has been given up. It appears a remarkable coincidence that the same padre who was at Arique at the time we were at Quinchilca was a fellow-passenger with us in the brig which conveyed us to this island. No sooner had he landed here than he deliberately circulated all sorts of absurd reports concerning me. I was come to disturb the minds of the.faithful, to make proselytes, &c., &c. It was gravely believed that I was a clergyman, some even affirmed 'that I was a bishop in disguise. But of all this I heard nothing except the exclamation, 'Padre,' as I passed, whispered by the peasantry, nor should have alluded to such mere tattle but to introduce a graver subject. In the course of a few weeks, Mr Lawson, whom we had known before at Valdivia, arrived here in command of a trading sloop, and called me aside to inform me that Manuel, the friar above alluded to, was now here, and that after we had left Valdivia, he had openly declared that it was entirely in consequence of his influence with Don Francisco Abierto, the commissary for the Indians in that province, that I had been thwarted in my plans of residing at Ranco. Notwithstanding this, as it was not yet the season for travelling, I was still in hopes of outliving, by a quiet residence here, every sinister attempt to prejudice me in the minds of the Chilotes, fully expecting that these foolish reports would gradually subside. In this, however, I was too sanguine; for no sooner did I commence to search in earnest for the men who were to accompany me across the mountains, than it was found to be altogether impracticable. A North American seaman, who was the only individual whom I engaged, and who, from some length of residence in the country, was well acquainted with the people, assured me that he found it quite impossible to get up the party required. Further inquiry fully bore out his statement, and made it still more evident that Friar Manuel had not laid aside any of his opposition. In order still further to prejudice me in the minds of this people, it was insinuated that I had, by some means or other, occasioned the loss of the consecrated wafer, which a few nights before had been missed!

" . . . . Having at last abandoned, with great reluctance, all hope of reaching the Indian population in the part where they are most civilised and least migratory, my thoughts are necessarily turned towards the south. Happily for us, and I trust, eventually for the poor Indians, the Falkland Islands are now under the British flag; and although the settlement is poor, and may never be much improved from its present condition, still it is the rendezvous of numbers of whalers, and the head-quarters of the small sealing vessels which frequent the straits of Magelhaen. . . . . Making this our headquarters, I purpose crossing over in a sealer, and, if possible, bringing back with me two or three Patagonian lads in order to teach them English, and thus prepare them to become interpreters to the missionaries who, we trust, may eventually settle amongst them. Who can tell but that the Falkland Islands, so admirably situated for the purpose, may become the key to the aborigines both of Tierra del Fuego and of Patagonia ? "

After this decision, the earliest opportunity was seized for the return of the family to Valparaiso, whence they sailed for the Falkland Islands in the following November, and anchored in Berkeley Sound on the 23d of December. This group of islands numbers about two hundred, but most of them are very small—the two largest are called East and West Falkland. The seat of government was at that time at Port Louis, in Berkeley Sound, but was afterwards transferred to Port William, where the town of Stanley has been built.

In December 1841, Port Louis presented a very dreary aspect. It was simply a naval station, under the command of Lieutenant Tyssen, of H.M. ketch *Arrow*, and he was absent surveying another harbour. A few scattered cottages formed the settlement, and one a little better than the rest was called the Government House. No cultivation varied the monotony of the treeless landscape, but the undulating plains were healthy, and abounded with wild fowl : there were also herds of wild cattle, which had multiplied from a few imported when the Spaniards held possession of the island, and the numerous bays abounded with fish. The residents on the island numbered only about twenty men and three or four women ; and the new-comers were much indebted to Lieutenant Cox, of H.M. ketch *Sparrow*, who rendered them every friendly help, including the services of a boat's crew to erect a small wooden house which they had brought with them.

A few months later, Lieutenant Moody, R.E., came as governor with a company of sappers and miners ; and in the month of April the society of the island received a great accession by the arrival of H.M.S. *Erebus* and *Terror*, under Captain J. C. Ross and Captain F. Crozier, who were on a voyage of magnetic observation and put in for the winter.

Captain Gardiner found it much less easy than he had anticipated to obtain a passage to Patagonia from the Falkland Islands, and was at last induced to charter a small sailing schooner to take him there. We give his own account of the trip :—

" The schooner which had been engaged for the purpose entered the straits of Magelhaen, March 22. 1842, and after a fruitless attempt to obtain the confidence of the natives, on the north coast of Tierra del Fuego, we anchored in Gregory Bay. Although this is one of the principal resorts of the natives, none were seen on this occasion ; the country for a considerable distance was examined, and at a spot, about eight miles inland, traces of a recent encampment were observed; but as no eligible site was found for a missionary station, we proceeded to Oazy harbour, about twenty miles to the westward, where a party of Indians, who were not far distant, soon made their appearance, and shortly afterwards formed an encampment near the anchorage.

" By means of an individual named San Leon, (a native of Monte Video, who had resided twelve years in the country,) they were made distinctly to understand that I came in the character of a missionary, and that my only object in visiting them was to prepare the way for their being instructed in the knowledge of the true God. They replied that I was at liberty to remain as long as I pleased, and to build where I thought proper : they also entered into an agreement, at my request, that none of my property should be stolen or injured. This I deemed expedient, from the number of Fuegians who were residing amongst them, and who have the character of being notorious thieves. During the time that the schooner was absent, procuring a cargo of timber in Port Famine, I had an opportunity of putting these fair promises to the test, and must acknowledge that they gave me as little trouble as any natives whom I have seen.

Shortly before I left the encampment at Oazy harbour, which consisted of about a hundred individuals, the principal chief, Wissale, arrived with about an equal number from the interior, having been absent eight months on a trading expedition to El Carmen, the Buenos Ayrean settlement on the Rio Negro, whence he had brought one hundred and twenty newly-purchased horses. With this party was a North American coloured man, named Isaac, who had left a whaler on the coast, and for the last three years had been living with the Patagonians. He has in a great measure mastered the language, and can make himself perfectly understood, which is not the case with San Leon, although he has been so many years in the country. Availing myself of this favourable circumstance, my objects were again fully explained, and Wissale was informed on every point. The result was perfectly satisfactory, and from the high character which Isaac gave of him, and from the open and friendly manner in which he received me, I felt assured that he was sincere."

In consequence of the peaceable and friendly demeanour of the Patagonians, Captain Gardiner was encouraged to believe that a good work might be carried on among them, with every hope for a blessing. It had been his plan to remove his family there, and himself hold the ground, (as he termed it,) till the Church Missionary Society could send out a staff of missionaries, to carry on the work more effectually than he could do. Circumstances afterwards induced him to conduct his family to England, and follow up, by his personal exertions, the letters that he had written from the Falklands. But his efforts were unavailing. The subject was considered by the committee of the Church Missionary Society; but Captain Gardiner was informed that the missions already established demanded more than the means at their command; and any attempt to form a mission in Patagonia was declined, though it was pressed upon them with the offer, that if they would select and appoint the agents, the whole expenses of the undertaking should be guaranteed for three years, and £100 a year afterwards.

At length, in 1844, a special Society was formed for South America alone, and it took its name from the country destined to be the scene of its earliest effort. The head-quarters of the Society were at the outset at Brighton; and very soon Mr Robert Hunt, the master of an endowed school in Kendal, was engaged as their first catechist to go to Patagonia. The committee very much wished to send out a clergyman, in the first instance, for obvious reasons: but four years had now passed since Captain Gardiner's interview with Wissale, and fears were entertained that a Chilian settlement, just formed at Port Famine, might exert an unfavourable influence over Wissale and his people, if further delay ensued. Consent was, therefore, given to the proposal, that Mr Hunt* should immediately go out, Captain Gardiner offering to accompany him, and to remain with him, till he should be joined by a clergyman.

The two Christian adventurers were landed by the brig *Rosalie*, at Oazy harbour, in the strait of Magelhaen, with three small huts, one for stores, one for cooking, and the other for sleeping, and every necessary provision for their support for some months. The wandering tribe, whom they came to benefit, were inland at the time of their arrival, and the *Rosalie* pursued her voyage to the Pacific, leaving them alone. This was in the month of February 1845.

They found, on landing, the hut of a Fuegian, who, with his family, seemed inoffensive and readily pointed out the place where fresh water could be procured, always the first consideration to settlers.

" A few days afterwards two Patagonians arrived, giving us to understand that they belonged to Wissales party; each of them carried a bow and arrow, and was on foot. Towards the afternoon the chief arrived, the only mounted man of the party His attendants were eight men, from six feet two inches to six feet seven inches in stature, and two women, one of them his grandmother, and the other one of his wives. They had brought with them a store of guanaco and ostrich meat, but this was deposited in our kitchen ; while at Wissale's request, biscuit was served out to them. The next day we did not expect them to dine with us, as some of their

---

* Now an ordained missionary of the Church Missionary Society in Prince Rupert's Land.

tents had arrived. Wissale, however, hung about the place, and when dinner was ready, I invited him to partake of it. Instead of accepting our hospitality, he sat sullenly in the midst of a small group of natives at a short distance from the house, with his mantle closely wrapped round him, and his upper lip covered—a sure sign of anger, among all the natives whom I have met with, whether in Africa or America.

" A pretext for his displeasure was indeed set up, but of so trivial a nature that only a determination to create a misunderstanding could have made it a subject of remonstrance. He soon afterwards mounted his horse, saying that to-morrow his people would arrive, intimating not very unequivocally that then he would avenge himself upon us. I followed him as he was walking his horse, and pressed him to receive a present of biscuit. Every argument I could think of was employed, still he proceeded, still I continued at his side, telling him I should not leave him till he gave me his hand. At length he relaxed a little, but the biscuit was a second time refused.

" On the 16th, more Patagonians arrived—men, women, and children—about seventy in all. Wissale and his son breakfasted with us. He had said :—' Whenever you partake of food, I and one of my children must eat with you.' There was room neither for remonstrance nor modification ; it was not a request, but a demand, and there was no alternative but to submit. That same day the *Commodore*, from Valparaiso, bound for Liverpool, put into the bay, and the captain and a passenger came on shore. While they were with us, I took the opportunity of recapitulating what had been said before to Wissale, requesting him in their presence either to retract or ratify the permission he had given, adding that, as an English vessel had now arrived, it remained with him to decide whether we should go home by her, or remain and endeavour to instruct his people, giving him to understand that, unless he promised to protect us, we could not possibly stay. He replied that we were brothers, and that he would protect us, adding that, after a short visit to Port Famine, it was his intention to return to Gregory Bay, and remain there with his people during the winter."

Nevertheless, on the very day of the *Commodore* sailing, Wissale returned to his sullen attitude within his ample cloak, demanding food on all occasions, as well as spirits and tobacco. His gusts of ill-temper were sudden and violent, and his whole bearing was so hostile that the lives of our friends seemed to hang by a very slender thread.

The *Commodore* was soon followed by the *Ancud* schooner from Port Famine, having on board Padre Domingo. a South American Indian, who had been trained up and sent, on the principle of the Propaganda, to be a teacher among his countrymen. He was civil, and so was the captain, even offering the Englishmen a passage to Port Famine. This was declined; but the growing influence of the Chilian settlement was so apparent that this consideration, added to the hostility of Wissale, led to the decision that it was necessary to abandon Patagonia for the present.

Captain Gardiner writes :—" My own observations have led me to conclude that a very great change had taken place in the character and condition of Wissale and the people about him. They are now a mere wreck of what they were in 1842. Instead of possessing 120 horses, they had now scarcely a dozen, and even those only fit to carry their tents from place to place at a foot's pace. The same men who formerly rode off at a gallop on their hunting expeditions are now compelled to proceed on foot, and employ bows and arrows, like the Fuegians. This tribe is now divided ; the majority of the men and horses were with San Leon. Wissale is evidently jealous of him. For some time we were in hope that this circumstance might have operated in our favour, by causing Wissale gradually to absent himself from Port Famine, and make Gregory Bay his more permanent residence. But we have seen too much of his character to place any confidence in his conduct or his professions.

" . . . . We can never do wrong in casting the gospel net on any side, or in any place. During many a dark and wearisome night we may appear to have toiled in vain, but it will not always be so ; the promise, though long delayed, will assuredly come to pass. We can know, no more than St Peter did, at what time or on what side of the vessel we are most likely to meet with success ; but this one word I will add, ' Having cast the net on one side, let us not slothfully or unbelievingly relinquish the work, but, committing ourselves and the heathen, whose souls we seek, afresh to the direction and tender mercy of our God, let us now cast it in humble confidence on the other side ; and who can tell but the same gracious Saviour who commanded success to the disciples on the sea of Tiberias, will vouchsafe to ordain strength out of our weakness, so that we shall have cause to admire the riches of His grace ? ' "

No sooner had the resolution been taken of returning to England than an opportunity of doing so was afforded. The English barque *Ganges*, from Valparaiso, made her appearance, and anchored in the Bay. In this vessel Captain Gardiner and Mr Hunt embarked for England on the 20th of March.

CHAPTER III.

WHEN Captain Gardiner and Mr Hunt returned from their unsuccessful attempt to commence a mission in Patagonia, great was the disappointment felt by the supporters of the mission. They were unprepared for so great a change as had taken place in the position of the tribe and character of the chief. If the missionaries had been able to remain in Patagonia, they would have supported them under every discouragement, but felt that an attempt in another part of the continent would be a doubtful experiment, possibly only an exploring ▓▓▓ey, on which they could not venture to expend mo▓▓▓▓▓▓▓bed for the preaching of the gospel.

Such ▓▓▓▓▓▓▓▓ which prevailed among the members of the comm▓▓▓▓▓▓▓▓ptain Gardiner came forward once more, with unsh▓▓▓▓▓▓▓▓ and said :—

"Whatever cours▓▓▓▓▓▓▓▓mine upon, I have made up my mind to go. back▓▓▓▓▓▓h America, and leave no stone unturned, no effo▓▓▓▓o establish a mission among the aboriginal tribes. ▓▓▓have a right to be instructed in the gospel of Christ. While God gives me strength, failure shall not daunt me." This, then, is my firm resolve: to go back, and make further researches among the natives of the interior, whether any possible opening may be found which has hitherto escaped me, through the Spanish Americans; or whether Tierra del Fuego is the only ground ιeft us for our last attempt. This I intend to do at my own risk, whether the Society is broken up or not. I therefore beg of you to pause, fund the money which belongs to the Society, and wait to see the result of the researches now about to be made. Our Saviour has given a command to preach the gospel even to the ends of the earth. He will provide for the fulfilment of His own purpose. Let us only obey."

This suggestion was adopted, and the funds of the Society invested in safe securities.

Federico Gonzales, a young Spanish Protestant, had been engaged by the committee to go to Patagonia. As this arrangement was now given up, Captain Gardiner offered to pay the expenses of Mr Gonzales, if he were willing to accompany him on his present enterprise. To this he agreed, and the committee presented him with £50 towards the necessary outlay. They sailed from Liverpool in the *Plata* for Monte Video, on September 23, 1845.

The "Gran Chaco" now became the scene of their researches. It is a large tract of country, inhabited by powerful tribes, bounded on the east by the rivers Paraguay ▮▮▮ rana, and crossed by the Pilcomayo and the Vermi▮▮▮▮▮▮ ye their source in the high land of Bolivia, a▮▮▮▮▮▮▮▮ araguay before its junction with the Para▮▮▮▮▮▮▮ direct method of entering the Chaco is to ▮▮▮▮▮▮ a to Corrientes, or the Paraguay to Asu▮▮▮▮▮▮▮ 845 the province of Santa Fé was in a ▮▮▮▮▮▮▮▮ and the Parana was not open to traffic. Ou▮▮▮▮▮▮ therefore set sail again for Valparaiso in the brig ▮▮▮pe, proceeding thence to Cobija, in Bolivia. They arrived at Cobija on the 5th of February, and started on the inland journey on the 7th. One month afterwards, Captain Gardiner writes from Tarija :—

" With a very few exceptions, the whole country between Cobija and this place is literally a desert. Nothing in Arabia could be more sterile than that part of the road which crosses the Atacama desert; and even after passing the Cordillera from Atacama to Rinconada, the whole route is unpeopled and desolate, without a single tree, and scarcely any herbage. From thence to Sococha, is a defile with high precipitous rocks on each side; at the base, strips of cultivation, Indian corn, figs, peaches, &c., in abundance. The road through this long and highly picturesque defile is in the bed of a water-course, which sometimes in heavy rains disputes the passage with the inhabitants; once the rocks on each side were too narrow to admit a laden mule, and consequently the trunks were taken off, and replaced on the other side. A road I can scarcely call it; nothing have I ever seen so bad, in fact, there is scarcely a road in all Bolivia, excepting that which goes to Potosi. At Rinconada we came in for the carnival, and were delayed five days. In all the way very kind friends have been raised up for us, especially at Calama, at Rinconada, at Sococha, and here at Tarija. At three of these places we have been lodged and boarded in the kindest manner, without charge. We are here next door to the Matriz, which was a college of the Jesuits. They had no less than twenty-two missions between Carapari and Santa Cruz de la Frontiera, all which, within about fifty years, have been suppressed.

"*Carapari, April* 22, 1846.—Last night only I returned from a visit of inspection among the Indians, and am now sending an express to Tarija, for medicines for Mr Gonzales, who for some days has been very ill with fever and ague. God has been very merciful to me here; I am in perfect health. What shall I render to the Lord for all His benefits?

" We arrived at the Pilcomayo on the 21st of March. The river was too high to be forded, and, wishing to cut the matter short, I engaged an Indian on the 23d, to swim across with me, and away we went, leaning together on a bundle of reeds. The current was full four and a half or five knots, but

C

we gained the opposite side in good style, the Indians all aghast to see that a white man could swim as well as themselves. The country, on the opposite side, is entirely in the hands of the natives, who received me kindly ; but I am sorry to say, all my efforts were unsuccessful to obtain permission to reside amongst them. There is a village, consisting of about twenty houses on this side of the river, where we might have stayed, but for the host of flies, mosquitoes, wasps, &c. It was perfect torture ; and on the very next day, the 24th, we were obliged to fly before them, and set off to return to San Louis. When we reached Carapari, Mr Gonzales was too ill to proceed further. I therefore hired a servant to attend upon him, and the mistress of the house where we are lodging being very kind, I had no hesitation in leaving him. I set out, therefore, on Thursday the 16th of April, and returned yesterday, having spent three nights among the Chenese Indians, and visited four villages of the Matacos. The house of one of the chiefs, named Maiki, where I slept on Saturday and Sunday nights, is fifty feet long, and about thirty wide : nine cotton hammocks were hung from the roof and posts, and I slept on a sort of rude stretcher. They are quite independent, will allow you to visit them, and supply you with food, but not to build or remain among them. I was in hopes of making one of these interesting villages our headquarters, but this may not be. The Mataco chief, Marrachi, would have given me leave, but that he was bound, he said, by his relations with his neighbours, the Cheneses, to act as they did on the subject. These Matacos are a wild people. Their houses are similar to those of the Zulus, but built carelessly, and the thatch merely thrown on. They cultivate the ground, but not to the extent that the Cheneses and the Chiriguanos do. Before I returned here, I visited some villages within the Bolivian frontier : at one of them, called Timboi, our farm is to be ; we cannot occupy it at present on account of

Mr Gonzales' illness, but all things are arranged for our going there as soon as it shall please God to enable us. The Cheneses and Chiriguanos both speak the Guarani language, Let this language be acquired, and we may itinerate on all sides."

While spending a Sunday alone among the Indians, he records his thoughts and prayers as follows :—

" By the goodness of my God, I am brought to another Sabbath, and am now in the midst of the Indians, to whom I desire to convey the knowledge of salvation by Jesus Christ. Here is a suitable time to pause, and seek fresh strength and guidance of my God. What mercies have attended me in all these long journeys! Why am I in health, and my companion in sickness? O Lord, graciously raise up Thy servant whom Thou has seen fit to afflict with sickness : restore him again to health, and enable him to go forward in the work to which Thou hast called him. And, Lord, vouchsafe to me the light of Thy Holy Spirit, to guide me in Thy way. Purify me from pride, engraft Thy love in my heart, and enable me to set Thee ever before my face. Graciously direct me in my present perplexing circumstances. . . . . To Thee I thankfully commit every circumstance and event, well knowing that without Thee I can do nothing; and what I may seem to do, without Thy blessing, will assuredly come to nought. Give me faith to take courage, in the midst of apparent discouragements, to confide in Thy promise, even when all things seem to be against me. I know, O Lord, that Thy word can never return unto Thee void, and that none of Thy promises shall fail, and that to every specific duty a promise is annexed. What should I fear, disappointments, confusion of face? It cannot be that Thou, who art holy, just, and good, shouldst set Thy servants upon a work, and that on the faith of Thy specific promises, and then abandon them to the ridicule and scoffs of an ungodly world.

Ah, no, Lord it cannot be : if ever I meet with shame and confusion of face in any work which Thou hast ordained, it will not be because of the failure of Thy promise, but the failure of my faith.   Lord, increase my faith : I believe, help Thou mine unbelief.   To Thee, O my God, I thankfully commit all, beseeching Thee to guide me in what I shall say; to influence the hearts of the chiefs to whom I purpose to apply; and, if it be Thy will, at this time to open a door in this part of the country for the entrance of Thy glorious gospel. And, Lord, should I be hindered, as Thy disciples were, both in Asia and Bithynia, may I not be cast down ; but show me, as Thou didst thy servants, Paul and Silas, in some way which I cannot mistake, where Thou wouldst have me go. Vouchsafe, O Lord, to hear my supplication, and show me clearly the path of duty.   Let the light of Thy truth shine on these poor blind Indians, for Jesus Christ's sake."

The sickly season had now set in at Carapari.   Many persons had left in consequence.   Mr Gonzales continued to have periodical attacks of fever and ague ; and at length even the captain's robust frame was prostrated by a similar seizure. They decided, therefore, on retiring to San Luis.   This proved a most painful journey, and is thus described :—

" I was well in the morning, but no sooner had we commenced our journey, than a strong fever came on.   Several times I was obliged to lie down, unable to proceed.   At last, I lay exhausted under a tree, perfectly helpless, unable either to return or to go forward.   There I thought I must have perished, but providentially there was a shed near, and though nothing but water could be procured, I was thankful for such an asylum in my state of helplessness.   Mr Gonzales, at my request, proceeded with the baggage, as it was necessary that he should reach the village of Sapatera, before his expected ague fit came on.   Two men passed the night at the spot where I was, and kindly supplied me with water, and on the following morning I was able to mount my horse and proceed to Sapatera. But I will not go through all the circumstances of our distressing journey to San Luis : suffice it to say that though we were only fit for our beds, we traversed steep mountains, by-paths strewed with rocks, and were often obliged to walk, as it was either so slippery or so steep, that the horses could not stand, and our saddles were continually slipping forward upon their necks. Often and often we both lay down exhausted; and when I look back upon what we endured, and what, by the good hand of our God upon us, we were able to accomplish in those three most trying days, I wonder that we could ever have reached San Luis. Never was that gracious promise more fully verified, 'As thy day, so shall thy strength be.' On the day after our arrival, I was attacked with dysentery, which continued for eight days, and brought me so low that I was obliged to keep my bed for a considerable time afterwards."

" *San Luis, May* 29.—I now resume my journal, which I have hitherto been unable to do. The Lord has laid His chastening hand upon me, and I have been reduced to a great state of weakness. I accept it at His hand, as a token of His fatherly care over me. During my illness, the governor of the frontier, Don Sebastiano Estensoro, showed us very great kindness. Mr Gonzales has had three or four fresh attacks of ague, but has now nearly recovered, which is a great mercy. Most kind and attentive has he been to me.

" *June* 15.—The governor paid me a long visit; his manner was most friendly, and a conversation took place, which, by the blessing of God, may conduce to very important results. I had previously understood that it was the wish of the Government to promote the introduction of English settlers into Bolivia, and asked him what he thought would be the feeling of the Government, supposing an individual were willing to collect together some of the Indians, and instruct them in the Protestant religion, in the hope of recovering them from their present abject condition? He said he thought the Government could not but approve of such a plan; and that in all probability they would give a tract of land for the Indians to live upon. After some further conversation, I explained fully our wish to translate the Bible into the Indian language, and to teach the natives to read, and instruct them in the religion of the Bible. He recommended that a petition should be drawn up, stating our object, and requesting permission of the President to carry it into effect."

Shortly after this conversation, our friends left San Luis, and went to Tarija, where they were hospitably received by Dr Cainzo, the attorney-general.

"*Tarija, July 25.*—The Lord has been very gracious to me, having raised me up again from my state of weakness, so that I can walk and ride nearly as usual, and feel quite restored, being only much thinner than I was. We have every prospect of good success, and are in favour with some individuals here, who are likely to forward the work in which we are engaged. But I look above these second causes, and desire to have my eyes fixed on Him who is the Author and Giver of every good and perfect gift, and who will not permit those who trust in His name to be ashamed of their confidence. Our winter here is delightful—almost cloudless skies, no rain, and the temperature about what it is in England in June. Dr Cainzo left on the 21st, to attend a session of the Congress in Chuquisaca, taking with him a letter to the British consul, and our petition to Government. We had arranged to go into lodgings, but he most kindly offered us his house, and pressed us not to move during his absence. We are therefore comfortably housed, and cater for ourselves. We have, since leaving Cobija, travelled 1061

miles, over, perhaps, the worst roads in the world.   We cannot fly about here, as in Chili."

The consul's reply was a very friendly letter of strong remonstrance, in which he expressed his decided opinion that,
though the Government was tolerably enlightened, the ignorance, intolerance, and vices of the clergy were incredible,
and their influence sufficient to frustrate any attempt of so-
called heretics to enlighten the Indians.

Becoming anxious about the fate of his petition, Captain
Gardiner left Tarija for Chuquisaca on the 22d of September,
trusting by a personal interview with the President to obviate
any objections which had arisen.   He was so far successful
that, whereas the first petition was negatived, he was permitted to modify it, and the formal sanction of Government
was given to his proposal, to endeavour to instruct the Indians who live beyond the limits of Bolivia proper in the
knowledge of God.   He conversed with several members of the
Government, the President, and the Minister of the Interior,
as well as his former friends, Dic Cainzo and Don Sebastiano,
and was so well convinced of the sincerity of their support,
that he considered the way was now open for missionary
work among the Indians, and that it was necessary he should
either remain in the country, to secure the step he had gained,
or return to England, for the purpose of urging on Christian
friends the importance of sending a missionary without delay
to assist Mr Gonzales.   He adopted the latter course, and on
the 12th of October left Chuquisaca for Potosi, where he remained till he had seen Mr Gonzales comfortably settled.   He
was much struck with the decayed appearance of this city ;
deserted and ruined houses were seen in all directions.   In
the days of Spanish greatness it had numbered 160,000 inhabitants, now reduced to 14,000.

The Quichua, one of the aboriginal languages of the country, is spoken by the Indians within the confines of Bolivia, and to this language Mr Gonzales now devoted his attention, so as to be ready, when joined by another missionary, to proceed to the frontier. There, it was hoped, they might remain, within Bolivian territory. protected by the laws of the country, and tolerated by a liberal Government, while patiently attempting to open a friendly intercourse with the natives beyond the boundary.

Cheered by this prospect, Captain Gardiner hastened to England. Under date of Southampton, February 8, 1846 he writes:—" Having once more returned to my native land, after an absence of rather more than sixteen months, I desire to offer thanksgiving to my gracious God. In journeys, in sickness, and throughout my voyages out and home, He has mercifully watched over me for good, and preserved me from harm. Lord, give me a grateful heart for all Thy goodness; may it be to me Christ to live, and then it will be gain to die."

It will be remembered thast e Society's funds were in reserve, waiting for the result of this journey of observation. Unhappily, now that the time for action was come, they were deprived of the valuable services of Sir Thomas Blomefield, who was compelled by illness to resign the office of treasurer and secretary. As the committee had also been weakened by the removal of some of its members from Brighton, the rest were unwilling to take the responsibility of a new mission, without first applying to the Church Missionary Society. Had the application been successful, the money in hand would have been transferred to the elder Society. The Church Missionary Society having again refused the undertaking, it was then deemed advisable for the committee to meet in London, thus securing the addition of several new members to their body, and the kind assistance of A. T. Ritchie, Esq., as honorary secretary.

Their first object was to send out a coadjutor to Mr Gonzales, and they were happy in meeting with another Spanish Protestant, Mr Miguel Robles, by whose aid they trusted that the preliminary work of the mission might be commenced, while time was given for increasing the Society's funds, and selecting a clergyman to follow.

But at the very time when Mr Robles was on his way to Bolivia, a revolutionary movement took place in that country, which ended in the deposition of the friendly Bolivian President. The difficulties which had been removed from the path of Gonzales and Robles were thus renewed. When the governing power was withdrawn, the influence of the priests was in the ascendant, and the society at home, not feeling able to cope with a hostile power of unknown extent, and to maintain an infant mission in the midst of the confusion which attends on civil troubles, reluctantly gave the order to their two agents to withdraw.

From the time that Captain Gardiner and Mr Hunt failed in the attempt to form a mission station in Patagonia, the former entertained the idea of an expedition to Tierra del Fuego. He knew that there, at least, he was beyond the reach of any antagonistic Papal influence, the most southern Spanish settlement being at Port Famine.

He never forgot this half-formed plan, even while engaged in his Bolivian journeys ; and when his first petition to the Bolivian Government was negatived, though he modified the petition, and made every possible effort to get it passed, yet his mind reverted at once, in case of failure, to his original plan of visiting Tierra del Fuego, as if the expedition to Bolivia were but an episode between the design and execution of the projected mission. Having succeeded beyond his hopes in making an opening for usefulness in Bolivia, he pressed on the committee of the new Society for missions to Patagonia and South America the importance not only of supporting and encouraging their agents in Bolivia, but of commencing a mission to Tierra del Fuego.

If he found it difficult to urge the committee forward, they found it impossible to keep him back; nothing could stop him. He travelled over England and Scotland to make known his plans, and invite co-operation. But amidst the conflicting claims which come before all who look upon missions to the heathen as a duty, it is not surprising that the pecuniary result of all his lectures and meetings was very small; and finding that all his exertions were insufficient to procure for the Society such an income as might provide for a well-appointed expedition, he urged upon the committee to make an attempt on a smaller scale, which would at least be a step in the right direction, and would result in improved information.

He proposed to take four sailors and one ship-carpenter, with one decked boat, a dingey, a whaleboat, two wigwam huts, and supplies for six months. He hoped by God's blessing to establish a station on one of the adjacent islands, where plentiful stores might be kept, while yet the missionaries might be near enough to the mainland for the purpose of holding a cautious intercourse with the natives. Staten Island, which lies due east of the most easterly point of Tierra del Fuego was selected for the scene of the experiment. This plan was finally agreed to. The preparations were made, and the men engaged. A passage was secured in the barque *Clymene*, bound for Payta, in Peru, and they sailed from Cardiff on the 7th of January 1848.

A very little experience in a very short time showed that this scheme was quite inadequate to the requirements of so hazardous an enterprise in so stormy a latitude. On the 15th of March, they sighted Staten Island, and stood off Port Vancouver on the 17th; but the wind being contrary, and increasing to a gale, they found it impossible to enter the har-

,hour, and proceeded through the straits of Le Maire to Lennox suarbour, where they anchored on the 23d. The next morn-hng, the little reconnoitring party explored the shore of Picton island in their whaleboat. Banner Cove was selected for the projected mission station, and they returned to the ship. But even this little trip was not accomplished without misadventure. Two nights and three days were spent upon it. The first night was spent comfortably on shore in their tent, and the next morning, after worship and breakfast and an exploring walk, baffling winds and squalls so obstructed their progress that night surprised them on their way back, and they were reduced to run their boat on the north shore of Lennox Island, and go supperless to rest on a sandy bed, covered by the canvas of the tent, which they were too wearied to erect. Next morning the surf was so high as to prevent them from launching their boat; and a scrambling walk by compass, over hill and dale, through forest and bog, was resorted to as the most hopeful way of getting food and shelter that day. When at last they were cheered by the sight of the *Clymene*, their troubles were not over; for, as they were expected by sea, and not by land, it was long before their signals attracted attention, and hours had passed, a sheltering wall had been erected, and a fire lighted, before the welcome boat's crew from the barque came to their rescue.

The boat was subsequently recovered without injury, and the *Clymene* sailed to Banner Cove. The storehouse was erected, and some of the goods landed; but the first visit of the natives made the fact apparent, that, without a place of security on shore, or a vessel large enough to hold their provisions and property, nothing could be preserved from the pilfering hands of their unscrupulous visitors. Reluctantly, therefore, but of necessity, the attempt to form a station on shore was abandoned, the tents were struck, and everything was re-embarked in a few hours; and on Saturday, the 1st of April 1848, the whole party sailed in the *Clymene* f Payta.

The considerations which led to the above decision are thus stated :—

" The few natives who are now with us, even should no more arrive, will oblige us to be constantly on the watch to prevent them from pilfering. While occupied in guarding our houses, our boats would be at their mercy; and, deprived of them, the only means of escaping from the difficulties with which we might be surrounded would be irrevocably cut off. From what I have now seen, it is my decided opinion that until the character of the natives has undergone some considerable change, a Fuegian mission must of necessity be afloat—in other words, a mission vessel; moored in the stream, must be substituted for a mission-house erected on the shore.

" A large vessel would not be required. I should recommend a ketch or brigantine of about 120 tons, with a master and seven hands. Provisions for twelve months should be taken out, but three-quarters should be deposited on the Falkland islands, when, as opportunity offered, supplies should afterwards be forwarded.

" There is no lack of wild ducks and other birds that would be good for the table; but, strange to say, they were found to be exceedingly shy, and difficult to approach. However, on the lagoon we saw many; and by going at the proper times, early and late, when the principal haunts are known, there is little doubt that any two individuals, who were tolerable shots, would bring in a sufficient supply, which, together with fish, would almost provide for the crew of a small vessel. The wastes of all these islands abound with seal, penguin, shag, loggerhead, and steamer ducks; and on the land brent ducks, upland geese, snipe, and other birds, are to be met

with. One evening a man employed himself in fishing most
successfully; the hook and line were scarcely down, when the
bait was nibbled at, and many fish were caught in a very
short time. While the crew were preparing for sea, I landed
with our fellow-passenger, in Tent Cove, taking the goats,
and some cuttings of raspberry, currant, and gooseberry, with
a few garden bulbs, which I had brought from England.
We then set to work with our spades, and, having cleared a
patch of ground on the Isthmus, set the cuttings, and deposited some of the bulbs.

" The anchorage off Banner Cove was found to be far
superior to that in Lennox Roads, and the cove itself affords
shelter from all winds for small vessels. There is no danger
in approaching Picton Island from seaward, and both wood
and water are abundant.

" The only obstacle which I can anticipate to the prose-
cution of our missionary objects in Tierra del Fuego, is one
which I am almost ashamed to mention, *i.e.*, *the expense.*
But ' let us not be weary in well-doing; for in due season we
shall reap, if we faint not.' "

In this narrative, an attempt has been made to delineate
the personal history of Captain Gardiner, without intruding
into the privacy of family life. Yet it is due to his memory
to state that, notwithstanding his frequent absence from home,
there are few persons whose individual influence has been more
lastingly felt in their own household than his. He was a
strict disciplinarian, and regarded God's approval of Abraham,
expressed in Gen. xviii. 19, as a lesson to all parents and
masters ; but the exercise of authority never lost him the
confidence of his children. Their first impulse, on devising
any little scheme of pleasure, was to consult their father,
being certain that he would enter heartily into it, and share
their enjoyment. He took great pains with their religious
instruction ; and while travelling with them in foreign coun-

tries, adopted some ingenious expedients for adding to their little stores of knowledge in an entertaining way. At those times also, his inventive powers were unceasingly exercised for insuring the comfort of his wife and children, while encountering the petty inconveniences of travelling.

The vigour with which he followed out his convictions is worthy of remark. With a frame of iron, and nerves which never flinched from fatigue or danger, he broke, with dauntless vehemence, through every difficulty which beset his path. He was always ready to meet the attacks of friends or foes, listening and replying to opposing arguments; but he was invariably steadfast to his own purpose. He never entered on a new enterprise without very much and earnest prayer for divine guidance. When visiting any of his friends, he generally found some path in the garden, which he paced like a quarter-deck, for hours each day, in the deepest study of God's holy Word. Whatever might be the breakfast hour, he was always up an hour before, for prayer and the study of the Bible. Such a man was not likely to be turned from his point. At one time, when the obstructions to his getting at the heathen population of South America seemed insuperable, it was suggested to him that there was another large unoccupied field open to him. The Bible and the Tract Societies had not then any agent in the whole continent of South America; but they would willingly give him a grant of books, and he might act for both. The idea struck him, and he paused to consider, but his decision was soon made. " No," he said ; " I have devoted myself to God for the heathen, and I cannot go back, or modify my vow." From this resolution he never swerved, and he was constant unto death. There were intervals of compelled leisure, when he could not carry on the great work to which he had given himself. At such times he took up any work of usefulness that presented itself. When in Brighton, he visited the poor regularly in one small district, where his memory was fondly cherished, and many tears shed at his death. He also made a practice of going to some of the low lodging-houses on a Sunday afternoon, to read the Scriptures to any little group that he found willing to listen.

When in South America, many were the Bibles and tracts which he scattered. At Mendoza there was no sale for them; but the books were gladly received as gifts, and eagerly sought after, and a kind letter of thanks was received from a reverend preceptor of the college of that town, for some which his pupils had applied for and received. He made a special journey into the Argentine provinces, and found a ready sale at Cordova, Tucuman, and Santiago del Estero. There was a difference of opinion among the padres, some making purchases themselves, and encouraging their flocks to do the same, while now and then a friar would be found to warn his hearers from the pulpit against the danger of buying heretical books. Still the Bible was nowhere proscribed by law. The police authorities, when appealed to, invariably favoured the sale. In Chili, also, which was generally considered a much more bigoted country than Buenos Ayres, or other eastern provinces, a formal permission was received from Santiago to admit two cases of "Bibles and religious books;" and though they were less sought after in that country than in some others, they were gladly received at San Carlos, in Chiloe. After every copy had been disposed of, there were some touching instances of people coming from a distance, and in vain offering high prices for copies of the Holy Book. The success met with by Captain Gardiner was undoubted. And it was the more to be regretted that no one since the year 1826 had been accredited to carry the Word of God to a people able to read it, and willing to receive it. The few English chaplains who were stationed at some of the seaports, were so fully occupied with the thousands who were their immediate charge,

that they could not carry out such a work as this for th₃
Spanish-speaking population on a large scale. There were no
authorised agents to go into the country towns, no colporteurs,
no chance travellers, as in Europe, to give their gratuitous
service. Our countrymen came year by year, in increasing
numbers, to the principal trading ports ; but we know of no
man who at that time cared to compromise himself by doing
anything which might be construed into an interference with
the religion of the country. Better days have now dawned.
Chili has followed the example of Buenos Ayres, and passed
an act of toleration; and our great merchants have shown such
an interest in the religious welfare of their own countrymen
in the Spanish towns, as, we trust, may result in much blessing to South America. And since the year 1856, Mr Corfield
has been the active and successful agent of the Bible Society
in Brazil and the Argentine republics.

CHAPTER IV.

WE must now turn to the final effort which ended Captain Gardiner's exertions for the benefit of the South American Indians. He had returned from Tierra del Fuego ardently desirous to induce his countrymen to send out another mission more efficiently provided than the last, with a brigantine or schooner in which they might keep their provisions, retire in case of difficulty, and maintain communication with the British colony on the East Falkland. He did not regard his recent attempt as a failure, but as a voyage of observation, showing what further means were required. He found few prepared to take the same view with himself, even among his stanchest supporters; but impressed as he was, with the firm conviction that it was his Master's will that he should exert all his powers to carry on that Master's work in South America, neither disappointment nor remonstrance had any power to withdraw him from it.

The question was submitted to the Moravian Church at Herrnhuth in Silesia, whether they would undertake a mission, for which their experience in Greenland seemed to prepare them. Captain Gardiner went to Herrnhuth as the representative of the committee; he was much gratified at meeting there some of the Moravian bishops and clergy from Africa, the West Indies, and other parts of the world, who had come to the synod, which it is their custom to hold once in ten years.

D

The proposal was fully discussed, and excited a deep interest, but the final reply was given a year and a half afterwards declining the undertaking. And now, two applications having been made in vain to the Church Missionary Society to take up the cause of missions to South America, and one to the Moravian Church, a similar application was made to the committee for Foreign Missions of the Church of Scotland; but equally in vain.

It was now clear that the committee of the Patagonian Missionary Society must either abandon all hope of a mission to. Tierra del Fuego, or adopt the plans of the ardent and disinterested man who pressed them upon their notice. They therefore authorised him to collect the necessary funds as a first step towards such a mission. In the course of his journeys as a lecturer, Captain Gardiner became acquainted with the Rev. George Pakenham Despard, of Redlands, Bristol, a man of courage, energy, and piety, and a warm friendship sprang up between them. When, therefore, difficulties thickened round the infant society—when money for the projected mission came slowly in—when Mr Ritchie, who had been indefatigable in discharging the duties of honorary secretary left London for Liverpool, and no one of the existing members of committee was able or willing to succeed him—Mr Despard was persuaded by Captain Gardiner to come to the rescue. In March 1850 the committee met once more in London, and elected, as members of their body, Mr Despard and those of his friends who had consented to aid them with their counsels. It was resolved, at the same time, that the committee should meet in future at Bristol instead of London, for the purpose of enabling Mr Despard to undertake the laborious office of honorary secretary.

As it seemed impossible to raise money enough for the execution of his original scheme, Captain Gardiner endeavoured to modify his plan, so as to combine sufficient security with less expense. He proposed, instead of a brigantine, to take two launches, 26 feet by $8\frac{1}{2}$, in which provisions for six months might be stowed, and two smaller boats to act as tenders to them. Believing that launches of that size would be quite sufficient to navigate the intricate channels of the straits, he spoke confidently to the committee on the subject, and was heard with the deference which his practical experience demanded. They knew that he was sanguine, but they knew also that he was not asking others to undertake toils or dangers which he was unwilling to share with them, or of which he knew nothing. They felt apprehensive when they compared his original plan with the one now presented to them, but he was so clear in his reasoning, and so confident of his facts, that a majority agreed to assist him in carrying it out. Besides, it is apparent to all, that about the stormy coasts of England and Scotland there are hundreds of fishing boats which are safely navigated by bold and skilful seamen. The launches proposed for the mission were to be of the best character, of good size, and provided with decks; while, for a crew, he proposed to obtain experienced Cornish fishermen, accustomed to navigate the Irish sea.

Again with patient pertinacity the unwearied man travelled over England and Scotland, but little progress was made in raising the necessary funds, till a lady at Cheltenham, being assured that the want of money alone hindered the enterprise, generously gave £700 at one time, and afterwards £300 more that it might be immediately prosecuted.

The party was soon collected. Mr Richard Williams, a gentleman practising as a surgeon at Burslem in Staffordshire, resigned his professional prospects to share its hardships. Mr John Maidment was pointed out by the secretary of the Young Men's Christian Association in London as the one man of his acquaintance whose piety, trustworthiness, humility, faith, and hardihood, rendered him fit for such a work, if he should be disposed to engage in it. Joseph Erwin the ship carpenter, who was one of the former party, volunteered to go again, saying, that "being with Captain Gardiner was like a heaven on earth, he was such a man of prayer." Three Cornish fishermen, John Pearce, John Badcock, and John Bryant, completed the party. They were men of high character and simple piety, who had worked together as fishermen, and lived together as Christians.

This little company sailed from Liverpool in the *Ocean Queen*, a fine barque, bound for San Francisco, on the 7th of September 1850, and two months after, letters were received from them, one of which gives the following account:—" As for our little mission party, you will be glad to hear that everything goes on most harmoniously,—not a jarring word has been uttered, and, as far as I can judge, but one spirit prevails,—a desire to serve the good Master in whose name we go forth, counting it all joy to endure hardship for His sake. May we have all grace to persevere unto the end. The mission boats, *Pioneer* and *Speedwell*, are highly approved, and cared for as if they belonged to the ship."

Soon after the arrival of this letter, the committee prepared to send out a second six months' supply of provisions, and every effort was used to find a vessel to take it. But though they had been successful in prevailing on the *Ocean Queen* to land the missionary party at Picton Island, they were now unable to find a vessel which would take the stores to that island. They therefore fell back upon the other suggestion made by Captain Gardiner, *i.e.*, to send stores to the East Falkland, thence to be forwarded by a vessel which, he had reason to believe, was sent monthly by Government for wood to Tierra del Fuego. This information was confirmed from what appeared to be authentic sources, and the stores were put on board the brig *Pearl*, which was advertised to sail for that colony in April.

In due course of time letters were received from the voyagers, announcing their arrival at Picton Island on December 5, 1850, after a long voyage. The incidents of the first few days are thus narrated :—

" Before we anchored, three canoes, with natives, were seen occupied in chasing porpoises ; and as we approached Banner Cove, to my no little satisfaction, five goats were observed perched up among the rocks. The crew of this vessel went on shore, and caught two of them, and I have given them to the captain as some little return for his constant kindness. On Friday the 6th we erected our tents, and slept on shore. On the 7th, we constructed a strong fence of trunks of trees, &c., round our position, leaving only one small opening. This night, and during Sunday, the number of natives increased. The party which we found here on our first landing were quiet and' peaceable, but not so the people who joined them. Their rudeness, and pertinacious endeavour to force a way into the tents, and to purloin our things, at length became so systematic and resolute, that it was not possible to retain our position without resorting to force, from which, of course, we refrained. For the present we must keep the stores and everything in the boats. As soon as the *Ocean Queen* leaves us, I purpose going to Button Island, and endeavouring to find out Jemmy, in the hope of persuading either himself or some of his relations to locate here; secondly, should we be unsuccessful in this endeavour, I intend to go still farther to the west, in order to obtain two or three boys from a different tribe, and to retain them for the purpose of learning their language. As a last resort, should we find the difficulties too great, we could easily take three or four lads to Staten Island, or to East Falkland, and after their language had been acquired, resume our position here under more favourable circumstances.

" *December* 18.—The *Ocean Queen* will probably sail to-

morrow morning. . . . Our boats are not too deeply laden, but
sadly encumbered, besides which, the leak in the *Pioneer* is not
remedied, as I had expected ; nothing remains but to lighten
her, and get quite to the keel. We know where the leak is,
and only require a proper place to unlade in. Nothing can
exceed the cheerful endurance and unanimity of the whole
party. I feel that the Lord is with us, and cannot doubt
that He will own and bless the work which He has permitted
us to begin."

Such cheerful communications were calculated to allay the
anxiety of friends in England. They knew that the stores
which the missionary pioneers had taken with them were
sufficient to last till June, and that they had also guns and
powder, besides nets for fishing. They knew that Captain
Gardiner had written to Mr Lafone of Monte Video, who
had extensive property in the Falklands, telling him of the
present effort, and requesting him to provide that a vessel
should ply periodically between the Falkland Islands and
Tierra del Fuego, bringing provisions for the mission, and
carrying back a supply of wood. A letter was addressed to
Captain B. J. Sulivan, R.N., at that time residing at East
Falkland, asking his co-operation, but this unhappily did
not reach the islands till he had quitted them. It was also
believed that the mission boats made a retreat to the colony
possible in case of necessity.

But as time passed, and no further intelligence was received,
application was made to the Admiralty for assistance, which
was promptly rendered. Captain Morshead, of H.M.S. *Dido*,
received directions to touch at Picton Island, on his way to
the Pacific, and left England in October 1851.   −

We must now follow the eventful course of the mission
party. The *Ocean Queen* left them on December 19 ; and,
according to the plan stated in the letter which he had just
sent to England, Captain Gardiner prepared for a voyage to

Button Island. But first it was necessary to disencumber the boats by depositing a part of the stores in some place of security, and to stop the leak of the *Pioneer*. On the very same day they began their search for a secure harbour on the north shores of the Beagle Channel. The one selected Captain Gardiner called Blomefield Harbour, as a "testimony of respect to his valued friend, Sir T. W. Blomefield." Sad experience too soon showed how imperfectly they were provided for the necessities of their position. The dingeys (which in a brig would have been carried on board) were towed by the *Pioneer*, and broke adrift the first day. The *Speedwell*, meantime, was in a still worse plight, and the spare plank which she was towing having got entangled in some kelp, she narrowly escaped getting on shore, and was saved only by the loss of her anchor and the timber. Two attempts were made to get into Blomefield Harbour; the first time, the *Pioneer* got there; the second time, the *Speedwell* got safe out to sea. On each occasion the successful boat had to return for her consort, not knowing what evils might have befallen her. The third time of leaving Banner Cove the weather became so stormy, and the wind so contrary, that they were driven for refuge to Lennox Harbour, and beached the boats there on the 6th of January. The repairs were completed, and the boats floated again on the 18th; but as Lennox Harbour was too exposed for the boats to ride safely at anchor, they proceeded eastward to Spaniard Harbour. Here they found a beautiful cove for shelter, which they called Earnest Cove, and a river which they named Cook's River, within a fine harbour. But on the 1st of February a severe gale blew with violence into the harbour, the *Pioneer* was dashed upon a rock, and her bows driven in by the jagged root of a large tree which lay prostrate upon the beach. One section of the *Pioneer* was hauled up higher on the beach, and with the help of the tent converted into a sleeping apartment. It might now have been possible, had the weather been mild, to proceed to Woollya in the *Speed-well*, with seven hands on board, five of whom were men bred to the sea, taking with them part of their provisions; but having in one violent gale lost their landing boats, and the *Pioneer* itself in another, they felt that it would be useless to make any further attempt with their present means. Not being able to go to Button Island, where there was some hope of finding a friendly, English-speaking native, still less could they remain at Banner Cove, where the natives were liable to come in large force, and were hostile to their movements. They determined, therefore, to wait in Spaniard Harbour till the arrival of the relieving vessel, which they had reason to expect from England or from the Falklands. The possibility of a vessel not arriving did not occur apparently to any of the party. The result of their consultation is thus stated by Mr Williams :—

"*Feb.* 2, 1851.—How evident that we were not in a position to commence with such slight means so arduous an undertaking! But all this is well; the mission has been thereby begun, whereas, had we waited for more efficient means, it never probably would have been. We are now all agreed that nothing short of a brigantine or schooner of eighty or a hundred tons burden can answer our ends, and to procure this ultimately the captain has fully determined to use every effort. Our plan of action now is to 'rough it' through all the circumstances which it shall please God to permit to happen to us until the arrival of a vessel, and then to take with us some Fuegians, and go to the Falkland Islands, there to learn their language; and when we have acquired it, and got the necessary vessel, to come out again, and go amongst them.

"A short acquaintance with the natives confirmed the unfavourable report which such writers as Fitz Roy, King, and Darwin had given; and in the forefront of all their actions it was visible that when they were the weaker party, they were mild and submissive, but the instant they had the prospect of taking us at unawares, they became presuming and full of mischief."

It soon became impossible to alter this decision, for within a few days sickness commenced. Mr Williams was the first who was seized. His disorder began with a severe chill; but early in March symptoms of scurvy showed themselves, the result of the want of animal food, which was occasioned by the loss of their powder. John Badcock was the next who sickened.

One more voyage only they made to Banner Cove to fetch away some provisions which they had concealed there, and to put up notices to show where they were gone. Then having taken all the measures needful to insure their being found in Spaniard Harbour by any vessel searching for them in Banner Cove, they returned to their retreat on Saturday the 29th of March; from this time watching for the vessel which never came, with that hope deferred which would have made the heart sick, if it had not been that their faith was made to grow exceedingly, and that they were filled with comfort in all their tribulations.

CHAPTER V.

WE now give such extracts from Captain Gardiner's journal as our space will admit, to show what intercourse they had with the natives, the means used to procure food, and lastly that wonderful testimony to the power of Divine grace which the concluding portion gives.

The first notice of the natives after the *Ocean Queen* left is on

"*Dec.* 23, 1850.—During the whole of Saturday, we had been at sea, and did not reach our anchorage till one o'clock on Sunday morning the 22d. At daylight we were awoke by the voices of the natives, two of whom were preparing to enter the boat, which to our great concern we found immovable, the tide having left her aground. We united in prayer. The two natives observed us, and as we proceeded they became more quiet, and at length seemed in some degree awed.

"Mr Maidment espied the *Speedwell*, standing out. No time was lost in putting her about ; but before she could approach, five more men made their appearance, approaching us by the beach. Taking it for granted that their intentions were hostile, considering the overbearing conduct of the two who had been with us since daylight, we landed with our guns and walked towards them, and when within a few paces, we knelt down upon the beach, and committed ourselves to the mercy and protection of our heavenly Father. They

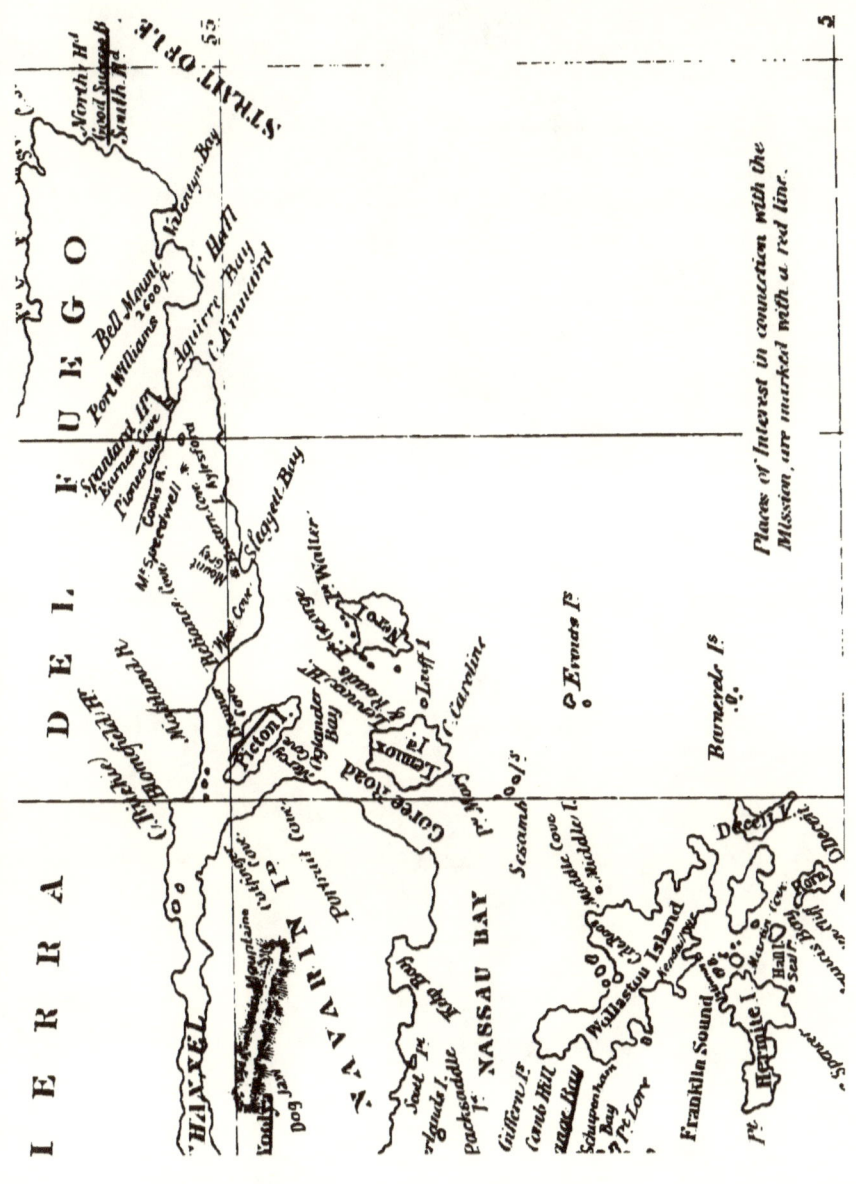

Places of Interest in connection with the Mission, are marked with a red line.

stood still, without uttering a word, while we were in prayer, and seemed to be held under some degree of restraint. Finding that they were peaceably inclined, some presents, such as knives and buttons, were distributed among them; but in order to be prepared, as our situation was still favourable for an attack, I walked round to a spot opposite to the *Speedwell*, and directed Erwin to prepare a raft, in order that as a last resource we might, if attacked, take refuge on board of her. On my return, we commenced our usual Sunday service. The natives were still standing close to the boat, and it was again remarked that, as we proceeded, they gradually became quiet, and their whole demeanour was greatly subdued. As soon as we were afloat again, both boats returned to their former anchorage in Banner Cove."

Mr Williams writes under date—" *Dec.* 31, 1850.—Two things have happened of a disappointing nature, which it has rather puzzled us to make up for. One is that whereas Captrocks, ardiner was in expectation of there being abundance carcelh here, we find literally none, saving the small ones caught by the natives, but we do not know where they obtained them. The other disappointment arises from our having left our stock of powder on board, so that we can no longer supply ourselves with ducks and geese, of which there are plenty here. Anticipating neither of these failures, no large provision of animal food was made—only two casks of preserved meat and one of pork, the latter purchased from the *Ocean Queen*—consequently, our diet consists chiefly of wheatmeal and oatmeal, with rice and biscuit, cheese, butter, and molasses."

We resume our extracts from Captain Gardiner's journal:—

" *January* 6, 1851.—After a lapse of nine days, the longest period during which the natives had been away from us, they returned about seven o'clock on Saturday morning, January 4.

They entered by Cook's Passage in different parties; first three, then two, and afterwards three more canoes came. As they approached, they divided, three going alongside each of the boats, while the other two remained near the wigwam, nearly opposite to us. On perceiving the three last canoes rounding the point, I gave directions for leaving the Cove, as there was every reason to apprehend that so large an assemblage of natives was for some hostile purpose, and not for friendly traffic, as the people alongside in the canoes were evidently desirous that we should regard it. They commenced by offering us fish for barter, which of course we accepted, giving them some articles in return. On perceiving a bundle of long war-spears in the stern of the two canoes which were near the wigwam, and the men in them deliberately handing to each other baskets of stones from the beach, there was no room for doubt or deliberation. The order to cut the cable was instantly given and as readily obeyed; our stern anchor was soon hove up, a   vere shortly afterwards under sail. As soon as we   airly out, and under the lee of the land, we closed in order to exchange some provisions, in the event of our being separated, and offered up our praises and thanksgivings to our gracious God, who had shielded us in the hour of peril, and so mercifully restrained the natives from carrying their design into effect. Had the wind permitted, we should have gone to Blomefield Harbour, but Lennox Harbour was the only one to which we could with safety steer.

"*Tuesday, March 25—Tent Cove.*—Went round Garden Island in quest of goats. Saw none, but found the skin of a kid which had been killed. It is therefore to be feared that the natives have killed them all. This is a sad disappointment, as fresh meat is now so essential for those who are sick. Yesterday, for a few nails, seventy fish were purchased from the natives. This afternoon we took on board the three casks of biscuit which had been deposited here, with the pork, a timely supply.

" *Wednesday* 26.—Moved this morning into Banner Cove. In the afternoon buried three bottles with notes in them, signifying where we were to be found should we leave this cove ; also painted a notification to the same effect on the rocks in two places. The bottles contain the following notification :—We are gone to Spaniard Harbour, which is on the main island, not far from Cape Kinnaird. We have sickness on board ; our supplies are nearly out ; and if not soon relieved we shall be starved. We do not intend to go to Staten Island, but shall remain in a cove on the west side of Spaniard Harbour, until a vessel comes to our assistance.

" *N.B.*—We have already been two months in Spaniard Harbour, finding the natives hostile here. (Signed and dated March 26, 1851.)

" *March* 27.—Went on shore to complete the paintings on the rocks, and otherwise notify the place of our destination. Had scarcely finished when some canoes appeared near Cook's Passage, and the voices of the natives were heard. Returned on board with John Pearce, who had accompanied me. Four canoes came alongside, very noisy and turbulent. Obtained a few fish for pieces of iron hoop. But notwithstanding all our vigilance, they contrived to cut our raft adrift ; happily it was recovered by means of our long boat-hook, on which they all, to our great relief, took their departure. They have taken up their quarters in the wigwam left by the party which went away on Monday.

" *Friday* 28.—Kept a short watch during the night, Mr Maidment and I taking four hours each. The natives were moving about at one o'clock, striking wood, as we suppose, for signals, &c. At four called the people to get under way, and by half-past four we were leaving Banner Cove, with a light air, and three oars pulling. The natives seemed in a bustle, fires had already been placed in their canoes, and they followed us a little way in them. In all probability there was a reinforcement near.

"*March* 29—*Earnest Cove.*—This afternoon we anchored in our old berth in Earnest Cove ; the passage was an anxious one, and fatiguing to the men. Mr Williams has borne the passage better than I could have expected. We have experienced the good hand of our God upon us in carrying us out and bringing us back in safety, and enabling us to do in Banner Cove all that was necessary for insuring, as far as instrumentality is concerned, the due arrival of the vessel which is expected to bring our supplies.

"*Monday* 31.—Rigged up our sleeping boat ; sent the beds, &c., on shore ; and Mr Maidment and I took up our quarters as before. I have directed John Pearce to sleep in the boat, so that there will be four on board, and three on shore at night, which will be a great relief to all.

"*April* 12.—Last night it blew in gusts harder than it has done since we have been in Tierra del Fuego. It is my intention to move the *Speedwell* on Monday, if practicable, into Cook's River, as it is too great a risk, especially with invalids on board, to lie here. Had the wind veered to the S.E., I fear the boat would have been driven on shore. Last night Mr Maidment, Pearce, and I, engaged in prayer for the safety of our companions, and our petition has been graciously granted. The Lord has been very merciful to us in preserving us all from harm during such inclement weather.

"*April* 14.—This afternoon moved the *Speedwell* to Cook's River. Mr Williams got up, and sat in the stern sheets for some little time enjoying the scenery.

"*April* 23.—Yesterday I went on board the *Speedwell* to stir them up to devise plans for catching fish and fowl ; recommended the net to be set up, with a tripping line, near

the place where sea fowl roost, to draw the net and to use
the balls, as the Indians of the Pampas do ; a set of these
balls are making. We have provisions of all kinds to last
us two months, but some are very low. I have directed that
the pork should bo used three times a week.

"*April* 25.—Our guntrap has at last succeeded ; the
fox has paid the cavern nightly visits for some time. We
found him this morning shot through the heart, in the endeavour to take the bait, which was placed at the muzzle of
the gun with a string from it attached to the trigger.

"*April* 30.—Ate a small portion of the fox for dinner to-
day ; his flesh had rather a fishy flavour.

"*May* 3.—Yesterday we dined on the remnant of a shag
found by Mr Maidment on the beach, and to-day we had a
fine fish for dinner. Five were caught yesterday by the net
at the entrance of Cook's River. This is very seasonable for
the sick, and we have reason to be thankful to the God of all
our mercies.

"*Pioneer Cavern, May* 8, 1851.—' Though I walk in the
midst of trouble, Thou wilt revive me. Mine eyes are unto
Thee, O God the Lord. In Thee is my trust, leave not my
soul destitute,' (Ps. cxxxviii. 7, and cxli. 8.)

> " 'Sweet peace have they whose minds are stay'd, ·
> Firm on the Rock in Zion laid ;
>   No anxious cares disturb their rest ;
> Whate'er of earthly ills betide
> Amid the storm, secure they ride,
>   Their souls in patience are possess'd.
>
> " ' Children of Him whose watchful eye
> Regards the ravens when they cry,
>   What need they fear or bode of ill ?
> They know their hairs are number'd all ;
> Nor can the smallest sparrow fall
>   Without their Father's sovereign will.
>
> " ' Though all around is dark and drear,
> Nor sun, nor moon, nor stars appear,

And every earthly Cherith dries ;
Faith bears the drooping spirit up,
And sweetens every bitter cup—
    A bow in every cloud descries.

" ' The Lord who gave may surely take,
The bruised reed He will not break ;
    He knows we are but dust.
The oil and meal alike may fail,
The whelming storm may long prevail,
    Yet on His promise we will trust.

" ' Whate'er in wisdom He denies,
A richer boon His grace supplies,
    A peace the world can ne'er bestow ;
Though nought remain, we 're not bereft,
What most we value still is left,
    The Rock, whence living waters flow.

" ' Then come what may, we 'll humbly wait,
His arm was never bared too late,
    The promise will not, cannot fail,
Though dark the night, the morn will break,
His own the Lord will not forsake ;
    The prayer of faith shall yet prevail ;
And we shall deem the trial sweet
That laid us waiting at His feet.'

" *May* 12.—Three fish caught in Cook's River. As the biscuit was getting low, and we may not altogether have supplies for more than three weeks longer, those who were in
health were to-day put upon short allowance.

" *May* 20.—When I was at Cook's River this afternoon,
I found Mr Williams engaged in prayer with the two who were
left on board. . . . . It is delightful to see him so heavenly-
minded, and so anxious to draw all around him to the fountain
of grace, from whence he derives such inward comfort in the
midst of his afflictions.

" *May* 22.—Yesterday was set apart for special prayer on
account of the sick, and for supplies of food, and the expected
vessel. It was in the following order—General Confession ;

Communion Service, Ps. lxxvii. and xxxiv.; 1 Kings xvii.; Ps. xxiii.; Acts xxvii. Collects 1, 5, 2, at the end of the Communion Service, and last two prayers of the Litany. Prayer for all conditions of men. General thanksgiving. Last Communion Collect. One of Roberts's sermons on Prov. iii. 11,12. Prayer for relief under our present circumstances, &c.

"*May* 28.—The net was broken by the strength of the tide on Monday night, but has not yet been hauled up, as there is too much ice on the river. Snow fell yesterday, and also in the night.

"*Pioneer Cavern, June* 4.—' Until the time that His word came: the word of the Lord tried him.' ' Wait on the Lord; be of good courage, and he shall strengthen thine heart: wait, I say, on the Lord,' (Ps. xxvii. 14.)

> " 'In heaven the Christian Pilgrims rest,
> Where all are holy, all are blest;
> There is no night,
> No sun, no moon could add one ray
> To that effulgent, endless day,
> Where all is bright,
> And saints behold with open face
> The glories of redeeming grace.

> " 'And why should there be night below,
> E'en in this world of sin and woe,
> Where Christians dwell?
> When Egypt felt that darksome night,
> In Goshen all was clear and bright,
> And joy could swell
> From grateful hearts, serenely kept,
> While judgments all around them swept.

> " 'Let that sweet Word our spirits cheer
> Which quelled the toss'd disciples' fear—
> Be not afraid:
> He who would bid the tempest cease
> Can keep our souls in perfect peace,
> If on Him stay'd,

And we shall own 'twas good to wait—
No blessing ever came too late.'

"*June* 10.—The net was recovered and repaired, and on Saturday night, the 7th, was put out; but so much ice floated down the river during that night, and on Sunday, that it was again torn, and indeed has been almost entirely carried away, so that repair is impossible. Thus the Lord has seen fit to render another means abortive, and doubtless to make His power more apparent, and to show that all our help is to come immediately from Him.

"*June* 12.—Mr Williams writes, 'Ah, I am happy day and night, hour by hour. Asleep or awake, I am happy beyond the poor compass of language to tell. We have long been without animal food of any kind. Our diet consists of oatmeal and pease, with rice occasionally; but even of this we have only a stock sufficient to last out the present month, or a very short period beyond this. The weather is very severe, with a deep fall of snow upon the ground. But this is not the worst feature of our case. All hands are now sadly affected. Captain Gardiner, a miracle of constitutional vigour, has suffered the least, and, if I listened to his own words, he is still none the worse; but his countenance bespeaks the contrary. Would it were not so! Mr Maidment likewise has sustained the shock of our circumstances very well, but yet great debility is now manifesting itself.'

"*June* 14, *Saturday*.—Five fine ducks were shot yesterday near the boat, in Cook's River. They were evidently driven from the interior by the late snow, and were seen in a large flock. This is a merciful supply. Mr Williams and Badcock are very weak, the disease having greatly increased.

"*June* 16, *Monday*.—Again we have had a merciful supply, five more ducks having been killed on Saturday evening. One shot only was fired on Friday and on Saturday, so thick were the fowl settled on the water near the boat.

"*June* 21, 1851.—'Be merciful unto me, O God, be merciful unto me; for my soul trusteth in Thee: yea, in the shadow of thy wings will I make my refuge, until these calamities be overpast,' (Ps. lvii. 1.)

> "'Lord, at Thy feet I humbly fall,
> And all I have to Thee resign;
> Whate'er Thou mayst in love recall,
> 'Tis best to lack, for all is Thine.

> "'Firm on the Rock of ages fix'd,
> I shall but hear the tempest beat;
> The cup my heavenly Father mix'd,
> Though bitter now, will soon be sweet.

> "'But should Thy billows o'er me break,
> When call'd to suffering, want, or pain,
> This our petition would I make—
> "Let faith burn bright, and love remain."

> "'Uphold me in the trying hour,
> Permit no murmuring thought to rise;
> Let me but feel Thy quickening power,
> And crosses I shall learn to prize.'

"*June* 28, *Saturday, my Birthday.*—'Who am I, O Lord God, that thou hast brought me hitherto?' (2 Sam. vii. 18.) We are now, by the providence of God, brought into circumstances which to the flesh are trying. . . . . But I will not be anxious on that account; we are in the Lord's service, and He is merciful, and full of compassion. Though He cause grief, He will have compassion according to the multitude of His mercies. I know that it is written, 'They that seek the Lord shall want no manner of thing that is good;' and again, 'Cast thy burden upon the Lord, and He shall sustain thee.' Whatever the Lord may in His providence see fit to take away, it is that which He himself has bestowed. . . . . Still I pray, that if it is consistent with Thy righteous will, O my heavenly Father, Thou wouldst look down with compassion upon me and my companions, who are straitened for lack of food, and vouchsafe to provide that which is needful, ... but if otherwise, Thy will be done. . . . . May I learn entire submission of my will to Thine; may every high place of pride be abased in my heart. . . . . Lord, I pray that Thou mayst be honoured in me, whether by life or by death, and that I may never depart from Thee. Uphold me by Thy grace, and keep me from anxious care, from murmuring and unbelief; and may the sincere language of my heart be under every circumstance, ' The Lord gave,' and should the Lord my God see fit to recall any of His gifts, and even to take away all, still ' Blessed be the name of the Lord;' He hath done all things well. One more petition I would offer to Thy throne of grace, O merciful Lord : I pray that Thou wouldst graciously prepare a way for the entrance of Thy servants among the poor heathen of these islands. . . . . Grant, O Lord, that we may be instrumental in commencing this great and blessed work; but shouldst thou see fit in Thy providence to hedge up our way, and that we should even languish and die here, I beseech Thee to raise up others, and to send forth labourers into this harvest. Let it be seen, for the manifestation of Thy glory and grace, that nothing is too hard for Thee; . . . . and hasten the day when the knowledge of the Lord Jesus Christ shall be manifested, not here only, but throughout every nation, and people, and tribe, and prayers and praise shall ascend, and a pure offering from the hearts of multitudes who are now sitting in darkness.

" *July* 3.—During the last few days we have had many trials, but our mercies have abounded. On Sunday morning, June 29 Erwin arrived before Mr Maidment and I were up, with the not unexpected intelligence of John Badcock's departure, which took place at about eleven o'clock on Saturday night. For some days previously he had suffered much from a difficulty in respiring, and had become so extremely weak that I had little expectation when I saw him on the afternoon of the day on which he died that he would live over Sunday. His illness commenced about the middle of March. He has been a great sufferer, but throughout has exhibited the patience and resignation of a true Christian. During some portion of his illness, he was distressed with doubts as to his acceptance before God, but these were entirely removed towards the close, and he entered into his eternal rest in a most triumphant manner. Shortly before he expired, he requested Mr Williams, who was lying near him, to join him in singing a hymn. He then repeated—

> " ' Arise, my soul, arise,
>   Shake off thy guilty fears;
>   The bleeding sacrifice
>   In my behalf appears.
> Before the throne my Surety stands,
> My name is written on His hands.'

And sang it through with a loud voice. In a few minutes afterwards he ceased to breathe, and his emancipated spirit doubtless arose from a bed of languishing and pain, a world of sin and sorrow, to those blissful mansions which the Lord, on whom alone he leant for pardon and justification, has prepared for all those who believe in His name. As it was quite necessary that the body should be removed from the compartment of the boat which Mr Williams occupied, I gave directions that the interment should take place. The grave was dug among some trees on a bank opposite to the boat After performing the last offices over the remains of our departed brother, we retired to the forepart of the boat, and as the day was bad, and we were all fatigued, we had no regular service, but I read the 4th chapter of 1 Thessalonians and then engaged in prayer.

" On my return from Cook's River on the 30th, the tide having risen to an unusual height, I met Mr Maidment in the act of making his escape from the cavern. He had been working hard, taking to the upper end all that it was material to save, and had just completed the work. We went first to our sleeping boat ; but, considering that she was in danger of being swept away or filled, as the tide was still rising, we proceeded to the Hermitage Rock, and there, being a little sheltered, we knelt down and returned thanks to our heavenly Father for the mercies which we had experienced. Soon, however, we were driven from this place of refuge, the tide threatening to hem us in. We then removed to the wood, but the drippings from the trees were worse than the rain which was falling. We were wet, cold, and hungry, and could not venture to sit down. When, at length, we returned to the cavern, we found it a complete wreck. The barriers of stones which had been raised by Mr Maidment with much labour was entirely swept away. We kindled a fire, and endeavoured to sleep, but were too wet and incommoded by smoke to rest. It was not till eleven on Tuesday that we could again leave our cavern, when, as the surf was still setting in, and the tide appeared likely to rise as high as it had done on the previous day, we agreed to make the best of our way over the heights to the *Speedwell*. The distance by the beach is about a mile and three quarters, and perhaps not more by the woods, but it was a very trying walk, and it was dark before we reached the *Speedwell*. What could be done to make us comfortable was done most readily and kindly. The next morning, July 2, we returned to Earnest Cove by way of the beach, as the tide admitted of it.

" *July* 4.—We have now been more than seven weeks on short allowance, and latterly even this has of necessity been curtailed. . . . . In noting down our events and difficulties, I would not conclude without expressing my thanks to the God of all mercies for the grace which He has bestowed upon each of my suffering companions, who, with the utmost cheerfulness, endure all without a murmur, patiently waiting the Lord's time to deliver them, and ready, should it be His will, to languish and die here, knowing that whatever He shall appoint will be well. My prayer is, that the Lord my God may be glorified in me, whether it be by life or by death, and that He will, should we fall, vouchsafe to raise up and send forth other labourers into this harvest, that His name may be magnified, and His kingdom enlarged, in the salvation of multitudes from among the inhabitants of this pagan land, who, by the instrumentality of His servants, may, under the divine blessing upon their labours, be translated from the power of darkness into the glorious liberty of the children of God."

About this time it would appear that a hand was painted on a rock pointing to the cavern, with Ps. lxii. 5–8 under it. The following are the words referred to,—" My soul, wait thou only upon God; for my expectation is from Him. He only is my rock, and my salvation; He is my defence; I shall not be moved. In God is my salvation and my glory; the rock of my strength and my refuge is in God. Trust in Him at all times; ye people, pour out your heart before Him God is a refuge for us."

There is no record of this in the journal, but Captain Gardiner's Bible has these verses marked July 5, 1851, and at the end of the Bible there is a reference to the same passage on a blank leaf, with these words appended—" *Pioneer Cavern, July 5, 1851.*"

" *July* 22.—For six days we have had no intercourse with Cook's River on account of the weather. I was there this afternoon. Mr Williams is wonderfully supported in body and mind. Mr Maidment is indefatigable in his endeavour to obtain all that can be scraped up to furnish a meal, and endures the cold necessary in procuring mussels and limpets, and wild celery, in addition to supplying fuel and water, with the greatest cheerfulness.

"*July* 28.—Went to-day to Cook's River. Mr Williams still as much supported as when I saw him on the 22d. Erwin was in bed suffering from eating the mussels. He has now left them off. They had all partaken of celery, which was now in better esteem with them. I had strongly recommended it when last there, and the beneficial results have already appeared. They all evince a true Christian spirit, and I feel assured that this present dispensation has been beneficial, and is working for our mutual good in the highest sense of the word. May I be more earnest in prayer for the fulness of the blessing which my heavenly Father designs in His present dealings with us.

"*July* 30.—Went to Cook's River. All better except Mr Williams. Yesterday we hung up a tablecloth suspended to the branch of a tree near our sleeping boat as a signal to any vessel that might come.

"*August* 7, 1851, *Pioneer Cavern.*—On this day eleven months we left England for this country, and have been graciously preserved through many dangers and troubles. The Lord in His providence has seen fit to bring us very low, and to remove many of the blessings which we have so long been partakers of; but all is in infinite wisdom, mercy, and love. These seasons of affliction are all appointed, are measured, and limited by a God of mercy, who doth not afflict willingly, but for our good. He knoweth our frame, that we are but dust, and will with every trial impart to those who commit the keeping of their souls unto Him strength sufficient for their day. How have I abused the manifold gifts of God. How unmindful of the daily comforts which I have

so unremittingly experienced, although unworthy of the very
least of them ! [Lord, have mercy upon me, a sinner. Grant
that I may be humbled under Thy mighty hand, deeply
sensible of my need of chastisement; that I may not be
tempted of Satan to repine, neither to despise, nor to faint,
but to wait upon Thee, in the posture of a suppliant for grace
to profit by this and every other dispensation of Thy providence. I know, O Lord, that there is a deep necessity for
this trial, or Thou wouldst not have sent it; and I humbly
beseech Thee to vouchsafe to me the full benefit which Thou
dost design in it. Make me to see myself in the light of Thy
holy word, to search and try my heart by it, and may Thy
Holy Spirit work in me the grace of true contrition, and renew
in me the graces of love, faith, and obedience. . . . . Let
not this mission fail, though we should not be permitted to
labour in it, but graciously raise up other labourers, who may
convey the saving truths of Thy gospel to the poor blind
heathen around us. . . . . Hasten the time when it shall
be said of them that they are a people prepared for the Lord,
and when Thou dost make up Thy jewels in the last day,
may there be many of them shining like the stars in the
kingdom of heaven, arrayed in white robes, and with palms
in their hands, ascribing praise, and honour, and glory, and
power unto Him who loved them and gave Himself for them.
Grant these my humble petitions, I beseech Thee, O Lord,
for the sake of my Saviour Jesus Christ. Amen.

"*August* 14, *Thursday.*—On Sunday last, the 10th, I felt
so weak that I kept my bed during the day; but anxious to
keep up as long as possible, especially on account of Mr
Maidment, I went to the cavern on the three following days,
but yesterday I found that the exertion of getting in and out
of the boat, and walking even that short distance twice in
the day was too much for me, and only tended to reduce the
little remaining strength which I had. To-day I am from

necessity obliged to keep my bed, with little expectation of again leaving it, unless it shall please the Lord in His mercy and compassion to relieve us, and vouchsafe the food which we so much stand in need of. I grieve for this, not on my own account, but because it lays an additional burden upon my kind and truly brotherly companion, who often beyond his strength labours most indefatigably in procuring what is necessary for our subsistence and comfort. To him, as the human instrument, I must now look for those things, as I am laid by, and comparatively helpless, and in his weak state it will be a severe trial and burden. But the Lord has been very gracious to us; we have been provided with food and fuel, and are in the enjoyment of many blessings, more especially in the ability which has been given to my companion to assist, and to provide for our maintenance, which he does often with great discomfort to himself, but most willingly. In all this I would desire to trace the hand of my gracious heavenly Father, who knows what I need, and has in wisdom and mercy seen fit to bring me very low. He doth not afflict willingly; there is a ' needs be ' in it all, and I pray for grace to receive it as a merciful means of calling me to remembrance, pulling down pride, and causing me to wait more implicitly upon my God. My prayer to Him is, that should He, in His abounding compassion, see fit to raise me up again to strength, and to prolong my days, I may have grace to devote them entirely to His service; that I may be more grateful for His bounties, and a faithful steward of all that He may vouchsafe to commit to my charge regarding myself, and all that I possess as not mine but His, for which I must give an account.

" *August* 25.—On Saturday afternoon Pearce came over, bringing heavy tidings. Joseph Erwin was fast failing, and had not spoken since the previous day. Mr Williams con-

sidered him beyond the power of human aid. Yesterday Mr
Maidment went to Cook's River, and found that he had been
removed from us, and entered his eternal rest at six o'clock
on Saturday evening. Thus one and another of our little
missionary band are gathered by the Good Shepherd to a
better inheritance, and higher and more glorious employ-
ments. Our times are in His hands, and He can raise up
others far better qualified than we are to enter into our
labours. There could not be a more active, conscientious,
and truly efficient agent than our departed and deeply-
lamented carpenter. Twice has he accompanied me to
Tierra del Fuego, and on all occasions proved himself worthy
of my highest confidence and esteem.

" *August* 27.—Another breach has in the providence of
God been made amongst us. John Bryant, who had for a
length of time been failing, died yesterday. No one was
with him at the time. He was in bed, and there found
about the middle of the day, having quitted his earthly tabernacle, and we doubt not is enjoying, together with our other
lamented and departed fellow-servants in the mission, the
fruition of bliss in his Redeemer's presence. John Pearce
was very weak. We are now almost entirely separated, as
there is but one individual here and at Cook's River to procure firing, cook, and supply the two who are unable to leave
their respective boats; and both should rather be in their
beds, than bear the toil and burden of such exhausting
labours. But the Lord is very pitiful and of tender compassion. He knows our frames. He appoints and measures
all His afflictive dispensations, and when His set time is fully
come, He will either remove us to His eternal and glorious
kingdom, or supply our languishing bodies with food convenient for us. I pray that in whatsoever estate, by His
wise and gracious providence, I may be placed, I may there-

with be content, and patiently await the development of His righteous will concerning me, knowing that He doeth all things well."

Pearce was so overwhelmed with affliction at the loss of the brothers of his adoption, that he could offer little assistance. The energy and consideration of Maidment only ended with life. On two successive days he walked to Cook's River, and performed the last offices for Erwin and Bryant. He then returned to Earnest Cove, and attended on his dying friend for four more days. On September 2d he left the boat, but was unable to return, and his remains were found in Pioneer Cavern. The following lines show his unfailing faith and patient endurance :—

> "'Come, O my soul, arise and dwell
> On everlasting love ;
> Forsake this transitory scene,
> And soar to realms above.
> Though the dark cloud has hid my joy
> By His almighty will,
> His mercies cannot fail to flow ;
> My God is gracious still.

> "'Although my daily bread hath fail'd,
> I know from whom it came,
> And still His faithful promises .
> Are every day the same.
> His words the same for evermore
> As when they first were given ;
> Yes, blessed thought ! they cannot fail
> Though earth dissolve, or heaven.'"

Feeling his end approaching, Gardiner wrote a farewell letter to his son, of which some extracts are given by permission. It is dated "*Earnest Cove, Tierra del Fuego, August 27, 1851,*" and begins :—

"The Lord in His providence is taking one and another of our little missionary band unto Himself, and I know not

how soon He may call me, through His abounding grace and
redeeming love, to join the company of the saints above,
where there are pleasures for evermore. It is my desire,
therefore, to prepare this letter for you, that you may have
the latest proof of my affection for you, and earnest desire
for your temporal and spiritual welfare. . . . . The next
point is your profession, and the time is now arrived when
this should be determined. It is of too great moment to be
decided upon hastily : it will be the turning point of your
life, and your future happiness will mainly depend upon the
selection which you make. . . . . There is but one method
of coming to a satisfactory conclusion. Spread the whole
matter, like Hezekiah, before the Lord ; ask counsel of Him,
and lean not to your own understanding. . . . . But I would
affectionately give you this caution. " Do not think of entering the gospel ministry unless you conscientiously feel that
you are constrained by the love of Christ, and the sincere
desire of winning souls to Him. . . . . I refrain from giving
you any advice on so weighty a subject, but will just place
before you, in the event of your entering the ministry, two
or three spheres of usefulness in the Lord's vineyard abroad,
should you feel inclined to take the missionary department,
which is indeed a delightful one. 1. *The Chilidugu Mission.*
2. *The care of those poor scattered sheep (our own fellow-
countrymen) in the Buenos Ayrian provinces.* 3. *The distribution of Bibles and tracts in South America.* . . . . Your
grandfather gave me this advice, and I repeat it to you. Lead
a useful life, and, I will add, take the Word of God as your
guide, and consult it diligently, with prayer to the Holy
Spirit to open your understanding; for it is not the mere
knowledge of its contents, however enlarged, critical, or
clear, that will carry you safely through the snares and
temptations of this evil world, but when it is received as the
sincere milk of the word, by which our souls are daily

nourished and strengthened: then and then only we grow thereby, and are prepared for the cares and trials of life, and are renewed in the inward man: thus we are enabled to adorn the doctrine we profess, and become gradually meet for that incorruptible and undefiled inheritance that fadeth not away, reserved for all those who live by faith in the Lord Jesus Christ."

On the 28th he took a tender farewell of his daughter by a parting letter, full of the most fatherly counsel, and on the 29th he wrote his last letter to his wife, from which the following extract is presented:—"I am passing through the furnace, but, blessed be my heavenly Shepherd, He is with me, and I shall not want. He has kept me in perfect peace, and my soul rests and waits only upon Him. . . . . All I pray for is that I may patiently await His good pleasure, whether it be for life or for death, and that, whether I live or die, it may be for His glory. I trust poor Fuegia and South America will not be abandoned. Missionary seed has been sown here, and the gospel message ought to follow. If I have a wish for the good of my fellow-men, it is that the *Tierra del Fuego mission might be prosecuted with vigour*, and the work in South America commenced, more especially *the Chilidugu branch*. But the Lord will direct and do all, for the times and the seasons are His, and the hearts of all men are in His hands."

On the 30th he made an ineffectual attempt to join the reduced party at Cook's River. There is no account of Sunday, August 31, but there are paper marks still remaining in his prayer-book, which point to the collect and psalms of that day. The diary also makes no mention of Monday, the 1st of September, but we know that on Tuesday, the 2d, the last words were written of the "Missionary Memoranda," which were printed entire in "Hope Deferred; not Lost." It is probable, therefore, that those two days were devoted to a revision of the Memoranda, which contains an "Outline of a Plan for Conducting the Future Operations of the Mission to Tierra del Fuego," "Fragments of an Appeal to British Christians, in Behalf of South America," and a "Fragment of an Appeal to Government for aid to the Mission." The principle contained in the plan is what has been already named—"*To convey a few of the natives to the Falklands, to teach them English, and learn their language, and to provide a brigantine or schooner of a hundred tons' burden as a mission vessel.*" The whole memoranda bear this heading:—"Missionary Memoranda, 1851. Written partly in Pioneer Cavern, and partly in our Boat Dormitory. Concluded Sept. 2." The last part of the diary is written in pencil, and is given verbatim:—

"*Sept. 3, Wednesday.*—J. Pearce was too much overcome with the loss of his companions to render Mr Maidment any efficient help on Wednesday last. Mr M. went over again on the 28th. Pearce still much cast down, and could assist but little. Mr M. prepared the grave, a wide one, in which both the remains of our fellow-labourers were laid side by side. Mr Williams somewhat better, but the unexpected death of John Bryant was a great shock to him, and he had been wandering in mind during the previous night. Mr M. returned perfectly exhausted; the day also was bad, snow, sleet, and rain. He has never since recruited from that day's bodily and mental exertion. Wishing, if possible, to spare him the trouble of attending upon me, and for the comfort of all, I purposed, if practicable, to go to the River, and take up my quarters in the boat. This was attempted on Saturday last. Feeling that without crutches I could not possibly effect it, Mr Maidment most kindly cut me a pair, (two forked sticks;) but it was with no slight exertion and fatigue in his weak state. We set out together, but I soon found that I had not strength to proceed, and was obliged to return before reaching the brook on our own beach. Mr Maidment was so exhausted yesterday that he did not rise from his bed till noon, and I have not seen him since: consequently I tasted nothing yesterday. I cannot leave the place where I am, and know not whether he is in the body, or enjoying the presence of the gracious God whom he has served so faithfully. I am writing this at ten o'clock in the forenoon. Blessed be my heavenly Father for the many mercies which I enjoy: a comfortable bed, no pain, or even cravings of hunger, though excessively weak, scarcely able to turn in my bed—at least, it is a very great exertion; but I am by His abounding grace kept in perfect peace, refreshed with a sense of my Saviour's love, and an assurance that all is wisely and mercifully appointed, and pray that I may receive the full blessing, which it is doubtless designed to bestow. My care is all cast upon God, and I am only awaiting His time and His good pleasure, to dispose of me as He shall see fit. Whether I live or die, may it be in Him. I commend my body and my soul into His care and keeping, and earnestly pray that He will mercifully take my dear wife and children under the shadow of His wings, comfort, guide, strengthen, and sanctify them wholly, that we may together, in a brighter and eternal world, praise and adore His goodness and grace in redeeming us with His precious blood, and plucking us as brands from the burning, to bestow upon us the adoption o children, and make us inheritors of His heavenly kingdom. Amen.

" *Wednesday*, 4.—There is now no room to doubt that my dear fellow-labourer has ceased from his earthly toils, and joined the company of the redeemed in the presence of the Lord, whom he served so faithfully. Under these circumstances, it was a merciful providence that he left the boat, as I could not have removed the body. He left a little peppermint water which he had mixed, and it has been a great comfort to me; but there was no other to drink. Fearing that I might suffer from thirst, I prayed that the Lord would strengthen me to procure some. He graciously answered my petition, and yesterday I was enabled to get out and scoop up a sufficient supply from some that trickled down at the stern of the boat, by means of one of my india-rubber overshoes. What continued mercies am I receiving at the hands of my heavenly Father! Blessed be His holy name!

" 5. *Friday.*—Great and marvellous are the lovingkind-nesses of my gracious God unto me. He has preserved me hitherto, and for four days, although without bodily food, without any feeling of hunger or thirst."

Here ends the journal. The following letter contains the last words of Allen Gardiner. It is discoloured by exposure, and torn, but for the most part legible. The following is thought to be the correct reading :—

"MY DEAR MR WILLIAMS,—The Lord has seen fit to call home another of our little company. Our dear departed brother left the boat on Tuesday at noon, and has not since returned: doubtless he is in the presence of his Redeemer, whom he served so faithfully. Yet a little while, and through grace we may join that blessed throng to sing the praises of Christ throughout eternity. I neither hunger nor thirst, though five days without food! Marvellous loving-kindness to me a sinner!—Your affectionate brother in Christ, ALLEN F GARDINER.

"*Sept.* 6, 1851."

" Here is the patience of the saints : here are they that keep the commandments of God, and the faith of Jesus Christ. And I heard a voice from heaven saying unto me, Write, Blessed are the dead which die in the Lord : Yea, saith the

Spirit, that they may rest from their labours, and their works do follow them. They hunger no more, neither thirst any more, for the Lamb which is in the midst of the throne shall feed them," (Rev. xiv. 12, 13, vii. 16, 17.)

Twenty days after the death of Captain Gardiner, a schooner, the *John Davison*, sailed from Monte Video by order of Mr Lafone, to inquire after and assist the mission party. Three times before he had given directions for vessels to touch at Picton Island, and if his orders had been complied with, the subsequent catastrophe might never have occurred. But his agents had failed to carry out his injunctions, and at last Mr Lafone, in considerable anxiety, sent the *John Davison*, under Captain Smyley, on a special voyage. On the 21st of October she anchored in Banner Cove. The directions painted on the rocks were plain—"Gone to Spaniard Harbour." The bottles were dug up and the letters read. Captain Smyley then writes:—

"*Oct.* 22.—Ran to Spaniard Harbour. Blowing a severe gale. Went on shore and found the boat with one person dead inside, another we found on the beach, another buried. These, we have every reason to believe, are Pearce, Williams, and Badcock. The sight was awful in the extreme. The two captains who went with me in the boat cried like children. Books, papers, medicine, clothing, and tools were strewed along the beach and on the boat's deck and cuddy. . . . . But we had no time to make further search as the gale came on so hard. It gave us barely time to bury the corpse on the beach and get on board. The gale continued to increase, so that it drove us from our anchorage and out to sea. . . . I have never found in my life such Christian fortitude, such patience, and bearing, as in these unfortunate men. They have never murmured, and Mr Williams says, 'Even in his worst distress, he is happy beyond expression.' "* Captain Smyley adds:—" It is the opinion of myself and also of Captain Nicholls that with proper management they might have gone with safety to the Falkland Islands, Port Famine, or the coast of Patagonia. I have even done more than this in a whaleboat at different times." But he acknowledges, in another place, that their doing so had been rendered impracticable by illness and want.

While this terrible news was on its way to England, H.M.S. *Dido*, under Captain Morshead, left the Falklands on January 6, 1852, and arrived at Banner Cove on the 19th. They sought in vain for the bottles under the direction posts, these having been removed by Captain Smyley. But the sentences painted on the rocks remained, and induced them to go to Spaniard Harbour. Captain Morshead writes :—" Our notice was first attracted by a boat lying upon the beach about a mile and a half inside of Cape Kinnaird : it was blowing very fresh from the south, and the ship rode uneasily at her anchor. I instantly sent Lieutenant Pigott and Mr Roberts to reconnoitre and return immediately, as I was anxious to get the ship to sea again in safety for the night : they returned shortly, bringing some books and papers, having discovered the bodies of Captain Gardiner and Mr Maidment unburied. . . . On one of the papers was written legibly, but without a date, ' If you will walk along the beach for a mile and a half you will find us in the other boat hauled up in the mouth of a river at the head of the harbour on the south side. Delay not, we are starving.' At this sad intelligence it was impossible to leave that night, though the weather looked very threatening. . . . I landed early next morning, January 22, and visited the spot where Captain Gardiner and his comrade were lying, and then went to the head of the harbour with Lieutenant Gaussen, Mr Roberts,

* The journal of Mr Williams has been embodied in a memoir by the skilful pen of Dr James Hamilton, and published by Nisbet & Co.

and Mr Evans. We found there the wreck of a boat, with part of her gear and stores, with quantities of clothing, with the remains of two bodies, which I conclude to be Mr Williams, (surgeon,) and John Pearce, (Cornish fisherman,) as the papers clearly show the death and burial of all the rest of the mission party. The two boats were thus about a mile and a half apart. Near the one where Captain Gardiner was lying was a large cavern, called by him *Pioneer Cavern*, where they kept their stores and occasionally slept, and in that cavern Mr Maidment's body was found. . . . Captain Gardiner's body was lying beside the boat, which apparently he had left, and being too weak to climb into it again, had died by the side of it. We were directed to the cavern by a hand painted on the rocks, with Ps. lxii. 5–8 under it.

"Their remains were collected together and buried close to the spot, and the funeral service read by Lieutenant Underwood; a small inscription was placed on the rock near his own text; the colours of boats and ships struck half-mast, and three volleys of musketry were the only tribute of respect I could pay to this lofty-minded man and his devoted companions, who have perished in the cause of the gospel for the want of timely supplies, and before noon the *Dido* was proceeding safely on her voyage. . . . I will offer no opinion upon the missionary labour of Captain Gardiner and the party, beyond its being marked by an earnestness and devotion to the cause. But, as a brother officer, I beg to record my admiration of his conduct in the moment of peril and danger, and his energy and resources entitle him to high professional credit. At one time I find him surrounded by hostile natives and dreading an attack, yet forbearing to fire and the savages awed and subdued by the solemnity of his party kneeling down in prayer. At another, having failed to heave off his boat when on the rocks, he digs a channel under her, and diverts a fresh water stream into it; and I find him making an anchor, by filling an old bread cask with stones, heading it up, and securing wooden crosses over the heads with chains." . . .

In reading this affecting narrative, the emotions which crowd on the heart and mind are various. We grieve over the disasters, the privations, the dangers, the loss of the gunpowder, of the boats, of the net, the unfriendliness of the natives, the trials of sickness. We regret the decision to go to Spaniard Harbour, instead of Port Famine, or any place in the straits, where ships are liable to pass; or even to the Falkland Islands, before sickness and exhaustion rendered such a voyage impracticable. Most of all do we lament that such heroic spirits should have been suffered to encounter such hazards, without, at least, a vessel large enough to carry their provisions, and protect them from insult. But as we approach the end of the story, all these regretful thoughts give place to wonder and admiration, and thankfulness for the grace of God, which was so strikingly displayed in not one alone, but all, so that they were examples to each other of patient endurance, and unfailing faith. They endured as seeing Him who is invisible. They suffered the loss of all things in this world without repining, for their treasure was above; and though the outward man perished, the inward man was renewed day by day, till the earthly tabernacle was left, for a home not made with hands, eternal in the heavens. Moreover, through the marvellous peace and calmness and steadfast resolution evinced by the subject of this memoir, and the wonderful preservation of the manuscripts, when no one of the party survived to guard them, it is our privilege to know more of their dying thoughts and last words than can often be attained when one is in close attendance in a death chamber.

It would seem as if nothing short of so startling an event

could rouse the Christian world into an interest for the
heathen tribes of South America.*

No one knew better than Captain Gardiner himself that
the means which were provided for the enterprise, and which
he flattered himself would have sufficed for the purpose, were
not what the service required. More than once he had distinctly recorded his views. But the plans which he himself
had devised were reduced to the lowest estimate, under the
delusive hope that, at the cost of a little more hardship to
himself and his comrades, the work might, at least, be begun.
Any spirit less ardent than his own would have been chilled
by the ill-success which attended his unwearied and un-
rewarded efforts. But the apathy of his countrymen did not
remove the sense of responsibility from his own conscience.
The spiritual destitution of South America was to him a
living reality, and the duty of relieving it was, in his eyes, a
pressing necessity, not to be evaded, not to be put off to a
more convenient season, nor left to another man's sense of
duty, but to be done with the best means, if possible, and in
no case to be left undone.

There is, perhaps, no nation in which is more fully de-

* In connexion with the above remarks, the following letter from
Admiral Sulivan, which gives an account of the lost letter, referred to in
page 54, will interest some of our readers:—

" *March* 13, 1865.—You will be surprised when I tell you that a letter
from Mrs Gardiner, written in 1851 to me at the Falklands, and asking
me to send provisions to Captain Gardiner, *reached me last week*. It was
in a parcel with other letters that reached the Falklands, just after I left
to return home in June 1851. They were sent back to me in England,
and have lain in an office for thirteen years. I have often expressed
astonishment that no one wrote to me about it. The letters were delayed
more than a month by the ship not sailing as intended, or they would
have reached me before I left; and they would have been rescued, and
consequently the mission would have ended. Is it not another proof that
their deaths were the appointed means for carrying on the mission ? "

veloped than in our own the desire to receive a return for labour bestowed, or capital invested, and certainly none which has more largely profited by its exercise. Was it an abuse of this principle which made Christians so slow to see that there was a work to be done in South America, because the labour required was great, and the prospects of success remote?

There is another principle, the very opposite to this, of which happily the history of our country furnishes us with not a few examples, *i.e.*, a self-sacrificing heroism, which risks everything for the sake of a noble object, which does not calculate cost or demand return, but gives freely that others may reap the benefit.

Our Divine Master has taught us in one of His parables that there is a Christian duty involved in the trading principle, and a Christian way of exercising it, but His own holy example was the self-sacrificing one, for though He was rich, for our sakes He became poor, that we, through His poverty, might be rich.

If we acknowledge that the heathen of South America, as well as of the rest of the world, are committed to the charity of the Christian Church, can we abandon the work thus heroically begun, and be blameless?

Shall the fortress be left in the enemy's hands because the Forlorn Hope has fallen in the breach?

CHAPTER VI.

THE MISSIONARY SCHOONER " ALLEN GARDINER," AND THE FALKLAND MISSIONARY STATION.

WHEN the news of this calamity reached England the sensation it produced was very great. Much blame was cast on all who were in any way supposed to have occasioned it; some sarcasm was expended on the system of Christian missions; but great and general reverence was felt for the heroic courage and patient endurance manifested by the sufferers.

The mission now seemed to be at an end, and its supporters were crushed and dispirited, when Mr Despard published far and wide his prayerful, unflinching determination, " With God's help, the Mission shall be maintained;" and this resolve was followed up by much vigorous exertion. It was not long before some friends of missions were roused to a renewal of the work. In 1854 a schooner, called the *Allen Gardiner*, was launched at Dartmouth, and sailed from Bris--tol with a staff of missionaries for the purpose. It was just such a vessel as Captain Gardiner had often wished for ; and the plan now attempted was what he had left in writing as consistent with his latest experience and advice. It was also identical with the advice tendered by the Admirals Fitz-Roy and Sulivan, who had had much acquaintance with the islands and their inhabitants—viz., to form a station on one of the Falkland Islands, and to bring thither some Fuegian lads, to teach them English, and to learn their language, and, till that preliminary work should be completed, to form no station on Tierra del Fuego.

The vessel was placed under the command of Captain Parker Snow, and sailed from Bristol on the 24th of October 1854, with Mr Garland Phillips as catechist, and Mr Ellis, surgeon, in charge of the projected station; and it was intended that a clergyman should speedily follow as general superintendent. Keppel Island, near the West Falkland, was selected for the mission station, and, by permission of the local government, taken possession of in the name of the Society on the 5th of February 1855.

A voyage was shortly afterwards made to Tierra del Fuego, and, to the delighted surprise of all on board, the same James Button, who came to England with Captain Fitz-Roy in 1830, was found living with his family on his native island. He had not lost his acquaintance with the English language, and was disposed to be very friendly; but Captain Snow did not think well at this time to invite any of the natives to Keppel, and after making them a few presents returned to the Falklands.

In the following year, the Rev. G. Pakenham Despard, honorary secretary of the Society, offered his services as superintendent of the Mission. He had a flourishing school at Bristol, which was the support of his large family. This he relinquished to content himself with the narrow income of a missionary, and the straitened circumstances of a settler in a new colony, who is dependent on the stores he brings with him for every comfort, beyond those which may be procured by the labour of his hands.

He sailed with his family and two adopted boys, in the *Hydaspes*, from Plymouth, on June 2, 1856, and was accompanied by the Rev. John Furniss Ogle, M.A., vicar of Flamborough, Yorkshire, who had already been a munificent·

benefactor to the Society,* by Mr Allen W. Gardiner, demy of Magdalen College, Oxford, the only son of the founder; and by Mr Charles Turpin, as missionaries; and by Mr W. Bartlett as manager of the Mission farm at Keppel. They arrived safely at Stanley, on the East Falkland, on the 30th of August, but a serious disappointment awaited them. Captain Snow, who was in harbour with the Society's schooner, refused to convey the goods and stock to the Mission station, and Mr Despard was therefore obliged to charter the *Victoria* sloop for the purpose; and on his return from that trip, as the captain still refused to acknowledge the superintendent's authority, and protested against his plans, Mr Despard dismissed him from the command, and took possession of the vessel. Meantime, Messrs Ellis and Phillips, who had spent a solitary eight months at Keppel, while Captain Snow was at Stanley and elsewhere, were much cheered by the arrival of their brethren, and all set to work with renewed vigour to build houses, make fences, dig peat for winter fuel, and contribute to their own support by catching fish and birds for food, and seal for oil.

The following year and a half was spent by Mr Despard in a succession of necessary voyages, during which time he left his family at Stanley. He first sailed to Monte Video, to engage a new captain and crew, and spent Christmas at Keppel, and gives the following testimony to the young missionaries who were under his superintendence:—

* Mr Ogle, after promoting the establishment of the mission by the donation of £500, and by his personal exertions, devoted his self-denying energies at a later period to the promotion of evangelical truth in Spain and Algeria, making his home at Oran. He was returning thither in the French steamer *Borysthène*, when it was wrecked on the 15th of December 1865. Pastor Laune of Oran, in announcing the sad intelligence of his death, bears this testimony to his character:—" He had neither the spirit, nor the heart, nor the tastes, nor the manners of this world. He was a Christian of whom we were not worthy. He possessed the affection and the esteem of all who knew him at Oran."

"*Keppel Island, Dec.* 25, 1856.—Away for the first time on a Christmas Day from my dear family, but, I would say, not from my dearer Lord. Went ashore with captain, officers, and crew. We had service and sermon on Luke ii. 10, 11, and afterwards the communion. I was invited to dine with the brethren, and did so gladly. No regrets were felt— at least none were expressed—that we had not such variety and delicacy of viands, or such domestic comforts, as were being enjoyed by our friends at home; and if we were not hilarious, we were contentedly cheerful. I think we may augur well from this, and from the fact, that men unused to bodily hard labour are out at 6.30 every morning digging peat till breakfast time. Common labourers might be employed to do it. Yes; but when the work was done common labourers would not avail for missionaries, and their cost is nearly equal to these uncommon ones. It should be understood also, that the little evening spare time our brethren out here have is spent in reading Spanish, Hebrew, Greek, Latin," &c.

Another time he writes—"Cheered by an acknowledgment on the part of a workman of the sin of his past life, and of an earnest desire henceforth to live to Christ. Mr Gardiner has been the honoured instrument of bringing him to this hopeful state. J. E., the Basco, reads his Spanish Bible with Mr Gardiner, and the latter makes use of his recently-acquired knowledge of Spanish to reason with him, and open to him the Scriptures. This is certainly the only opportunity the poor man ever enjoyed of hearing God speak for Himself in His Word. The good God take note of this stray one. It is much for Mr Gardiner, in his efforts for these men, that his unvarying kindness and affability have won the good opinion of them all."

We pass over, for the sake of brevity, the account of Mr Despard's first voyage to Patagonia, of which he speaks under date Feb. 4, 1857, as "this land, which has so long been in my mind, and certainly in my prayers." Of his first voyage to Tierra del Fuego he says,—"I have lived to realise a long-cherished wish. I have seen the last resting-place of our seven brethren, who died in faith and hope of a heavenly home, and have felt my spirit stirred in me to desire and to pray for similar devotedness and uncomplaining patience."

Some particulars of this visit are supplied by Mr Gardiner.

"*Spaniard Harbour, April* 16.—About 5 p.m. we ran into this harbour. We put off in the boat, the first mate and I taking two of the oars. The captain steered straight for the mouth of the cave. The waves break into it at high water, and the surf on the rock in a gale of wind must be truly awful. We landed a few yards off on the beach. With a lighted candle we walked on and on till we ascended into a gloomy chamber. There is the fireplace where poor Maidment's bones were found; beyond is a gloomy cavern; while in front is the breakwater, which the waves have broken in upon. I left the cavern to search for the painted words, Psalm lxii. 5–8. Yes; there they were still, just outside the entrance, quite distinct and legible. Some pieces of the *Pioneer* mark the spot where she was stranded. The big tree, against which she was dashed, was there still, and the flagstaff, which has tumbled down.

"*April* 17.—We rowed to Cook's River, saw the remains of the *Speedwell*, and Mr Despard held our morning worship by the group of trees where we suppose Badcock to have been buried.

"*April* 19, *Sunday.*—Asked the captain for the gig, and landed alone to take a last look at Pioneer Cavern, and my father's grave. On the headstone is painted 'Captain Gardiner;' on a smaller one at the foot, 'H.M.S. *Dido.*'

"*April* 23.—Very heavy gale from the S.W. last night.

It is still blowing hard, and the snow is settling deeper on the hills. When the hurricane squalls come down, they make the schooner dance like a child in a passion.

"*April* 25, *Saturday*.—Thank God, this truly awful gale is at length breaking up. It must have been a similar gale to this which poor Mr Williams so feelingly describes. The same hand which kept the *Speedwell* from dragging her anchors on that night was also present with us.

"*April* 27.—The storm came on again on Saturday evening in all its vehemence, and the night was indeed a fearful one. This harbour is unsheltered, and exposed to the whole drift of the ocean from S.E. and E. Our situation on Sunday morning was a very anxious one. A heavy sea came rolling into the harbour, the wind hauling more to the eastward. But we were not forsaken. A sudden break in the threatening clouds was followed by a perceptible improvement in the weather: so mercifully did the Lord 'stay His rough wind in the day of His east wind.' In a few hours the gale was entirely over.

"*Banner Cove*.—We got under way from Spaniard Harbour at seven o'clock on Monday morning, and anchored here at one on Wednesday morning, having accomplished thirty-two miles in forty hours. I went below, extremely thankful for such a snug berth as Banner Cove. After dinner, the captain and I pushed off in the gig, and rowed to the rock at the entrance, on which is painted quite legibly, 'Gone to Spaniard Harbour.' The other distressing words are now hardly traceable. The scenery of Banner Cove is beautiful. Every one on board is charmed with it."

After loading the schooner with poles from the woods, and visiting Blomefield and Lennox Harbours, where they had friendly interviews with the natives, they returned to the Falklands on the 16th of May.

Mr Despard still had to take two more voyages, one to Rio

Janeiro, for building materials, &c., and another to Monte Video for a crew, the former crew having been unwilling to engage themselves for more than a single year. On this occasion he speaks most gratefully of the considerate kindness of the British consul, by whose means the usual fees were remitted, and every help given him in consideration of the benevolent object to which the ship was devoted.

At last, in January 1858, he settled his family in Keppel Island, and remained with them a few months ; the next voyages to Patagonia and Tierra del Fuego being undertaken by Mr Gardiner and Mr Turpin. The voyage to Tierra del Fuego proved very interesting, though a succession of contrary winds and gales delayed them much, and it was midwinter before they approached Woollya, in Navarin Island, where they hoped to find James Button. On the 6th, Mr Gardiner writes :—" Our time is up on Wednesday, and we have had no fair wind. ' O Lord undertake for me, and send us prosperity at the last.'

" *June* 9, *Woollya.*—It was a regular winter morning, snow lying on the deck, and drifting into the sails and rigging, the wind fitful, howling, and gusty. About 8 A.M. it cleared a little, and we were soon running before a stiff southerly breeze for Woollya. The snow squalls were very frequent, and at times completely hid the land. About 2 P.M. we were abreast of Button Island, and ran for the cove at Woollya, where Captain Fitz-Roy landed Matthews. There were two canoes in the cove. One of the natives sang out as we came in, ' Hillo, hoy, hoy.' I asked him for Jemmy Button, and he pointed to the island.

" *June* 10.—One of the canoes left about 5 A.M. this morning, and returned about 11 A.M., with four more canoes from Button Island. They soon came alongside, and made us understand that Jemmy's daughter was there, but he was over at the island. I gave them all some presents, and showed them the things for Jemmy, which excited their curiosity, and very soon his daughter started away in quest of her father.

"*June* 11.—A lovely winter morning, the sun shining brightly upon the frosty ground, and the surrounding high land dazzling white with snow. About 9 A.M. four canoes were seen rounding the north point of Button Island, and coming across the sound. As soon as they were within hailing distance, I sang out, 'Jemmy Button,' when a man stood up in the foremost canoe, and answered, 'Yes, sir.' In a few minutes the identical man came up the ladder and shook hands with me; he said his girl, as he called his daughter, had been paddling half the night to find him, as he was 'long, long, way.' She looked quite exhausted, but appeared pleased with the presents I gave her, as a reward for her exertions. Jemmy came down into the cabin and partook of some coffee and bread and butter. He remembered Captain Fitz-Roy perfectly, seemed much pleased at Mr Bynoe's remembrance, and the useful carpenter's tools he had sent him. I went ashore with Jemmy, and helped him to cut some poles to repair his wigwam. There were two other natives cutting at the same place, and I was surprised at their dexterity with the very rude tools they had. It was a picturesque scene, eleven canoes at the edge of the beach, and the natives cutting wood, some repairing their wigwams with green branches, and others lighting their fires. Jemmy gave his own people a very good character. He gave me an account of a tragedy that happened, he says, not long since. A ship, with English, fell among the natives of another tribe, and were all killed. This was probably a shipwrecked crew in a boat, and, perhaps, may help to explain why shipwrecked sailors are so often picked up on the Falklands, and sometimes on Staten Island, but never from the islands of Tierra del Fuego.

" *June* 12.—A perfectly calm day. Jemmy came off about nine o'clock with his little boy. Both attended our prayers. He said he would come with us, and bring his wife and two children. To try if he were serious, I proposed to send his canoe on board this afternoon, to which he agreed. Accordingly, after dinner, he told those who were in his canoe to get out, and I took them on shore in the boat. When the canoe was hoisted up, without being injured, Jemmy said, 'I go 'way, wigwam sleep to-night, to-morrow bring wife, go 'way.' He leaves his presents on board. All his tribe are here, and are very civil, both on shore and alongside. The men appear to make the wigwams and the canoes, to cut wood for firing, and to go after seal or porpoises. The women paddle the canoes, do the fishing, and make the bark cups and baskets.

" *June* 13, *Sunday.*—Jemmy came off this morning, and fifteen canoes with him, probably thinking he was going to leave them. Before service, I told Jemmy to tell his people it was Sunday, and ask them to leave the vessel's side. He went to the gangway, and instead of reasoning with them in their own language, as I expected, said abruptly, ' You go 'way, church, by and by, no go to-day.' This had the desired effect, however, for they all went away. What a change of events the last week has brought about! It seems like a dream, to watch the Indian fires, shining like stars in the water, in the dark night, and to hear the occasional barking of the dogs, reminding us we are in the centre of an Indian village.

"*June* 15.—Got under way this morning with a light breeze. Jemmy's relations were all alongside to see him off. After a time the wind died away, and very reluctantly the captain had to return to our anchorage at 2 P.M. Two canoes of 'bad men,' as Jemmy called them, came across this evening, and tried to get things from the rest. Jemmy said, ' Bad men fight,' and it really looked very like it. However, after a time the hostile party went away, but both sides yelled for ever so long.

"*June* 16.—I am rather glad we had to put back to Woollya yesterday, as it gave Jemmy an opportunity of returning to his wigwam if his resolution were shaken. But they all stepped on board very contentedly. This morning we left for good."

Eight days after this they were at anchor off Keppel Island, and were warmly greeted by their friends.

On the arrival of the Fuegians Mr Despard writes :—"*June* 26, 1858.—Mr Gardiner will be in England as soon as this letter, and will give you a full account of his voyages. The last is, indeed, by far the most interesting; and the result of it made my heart sing for joy and hope—James Button, his wife and three children, living here! You will hear that others would have come if allowed. We shall set every ear and tongue to catch the Fuegian language in these six months, so that when Jemmy returns we may be able to say something in it, and I pray God fervently to open their hearts and give entrance to His truth."

Mrs Despard writes on the same occasion :—"*June* 28th. —Rejoice with me, for the Lord has seen fit to give an answer to the daily prayers addressed to Him, the Sovereign Disposer of all hearts, that He would be pleased to put it into the mind of some of those poor benighted Fuegians to trust themselves to our hands and come over to us here. This important event in our missionary life has just taken place. On Thursday last, soon after breakfast, the delightful cry resounded through the house, ' The *Allen Gardiner* is coming in.' I ran quickly to the house door, from which we command a fine sea view, and there, truly, was the stout little craft, which has so bravely stood many a severe and stormy gale, rapidly scudding before the wind. Soon after, Captain Bunt and Mr Turpin came to Sulivan House, with the joyful

news that James Button with his wife and three children
were on board.   Then arose a shout of joy and praise among
us.   It is wonderful how well James Button remembers his
English.   He seems quite at home with us all, and came up
with his eldest child, a boy of eight or nine.   I asked him
his name, he answered 'Threeboys,' for what reason we cannot yet find out.   This boy is apparently very quick, and has
picked up many English words.   We long to make them understand something of God, and of that Saviour who came
down to save their souls; but it will be, of course, some time
ere they can be made to understand it.   We are doing our
best to learn as many Fuegian words as we can, but this is
difficult to accomplish, as these people do not like to speak
their language before us, and converse with each other in a
whisper."

The Fuegian family remained at the station till the
month of November, when, according to promise, Mr Despard conducted them back to their own country in the
Allen Gardiner, under Mr Fell, the new captain.   Mrs Despard writes,—" My husband left us on the 16th, accompanied
by Messrs Phillips and Turpin, and the Button family for
Tierra del Fuego.   I cannot tell you how we miss our late
guests, now they are gone.   During their stay here they behaved extremely well, never doing anything to offend or an-
noy us.   As to Jemmy, his politeness was extreme; and I
ever found him most grateful.   For any little trifle I gave
him, he would go and pick me a beautiful bouquet of wild
flowers, or spear me some fish.   He was always clean.   He
quickly recovered his English, and understood us better than
we understood him.   He knows that there is a God who has
created all things.   He also knows about our blessed Saviour.
I said, ' Jemmy, will you come back to us ? '   He would not
promise, but replied, ' Perhaps, by and by, me no tell now!.'
The Fuegians are very curious, and watch all we do; they

are also very idle. When the Buttons first came here they would not even fetch wood for their fire, although it was placed a few yards from their door. One day I said, 'James, God loves good men—good men no idle. God no love idle men.' He nodded in his peculiar way to show me he understood. A short time after he was hard at work."

Mr Despard returned to the mission station in due course, bringing with him three men and their wives, two boys, and a little child. He writes, under date of *Jan.* 23, 1859 :—

" James Button and his family spent the winter and spring with us, and gained much in our esteem, and we secured his confidence. I took him back to his home, and with two catechists remained a month at the place. We constructed a house in the English fashion in their country, and had not the slightest difficulty in persuading three men, with their wives and two youths, to come hither with us.

" *Oct.* 4.—You see how long my letter has been on the stocks, nearly nine months. One matter of urgent business or another has prevented its launch till now. Those same Fuegians are now just returning to their own home. They will leave us, we hope, to-morrow, and are greatly changed in manners. The two lads, Lucca-enges and Okokko-enges, are quite polite. ' If you please,' ' Thank you,' ' Good morning,' are ever heard in the right time and place. They give thanks at their meals, and pray at their bedside. Lucca is improving fast in writing. I could not but feel well-pleased to see the little brown boy under the instruction of my children. The carpenter tells me Lucca sawed some wood very well, and was much pleased with his hard work. Like a child, he thinks himself already a proficient, and says he is going to make a table and chair for his father. Bartlett is loud in his praises of Okokko. The men are also much improved. They have behaved in a very orderly manner, very seldom missed coming to daily worship, and generally twice on Sunday. They are now decent in their habits, tidily dressed, and as far as our imperfect medium of communication goes, they have been taught the knowledge of God. I have got nearly a thousand words of Tekenica, but am still a long way from ability to make a grammar of it. I have discovered neither conjunction, preposition, mood, nor tense in it. No word has appeared for God, or Creator, or pray. They have a word for Spirit, and they are very uneasy at hearing it, for they say they shall see it if named. What a comfort do we enjoy in knowing that God is the author of language, and has appointed that all tongues shall declare His glory."

It was the 6th of October 1859 when Mr Phillips went on board with his charges, and sailed for Stanley, where they stayed a few days, and set sail for Woollya on the 11th. Mr Despard's written instructions were as follows :—

" MY DEAR MR PHILLIPS,—I hereby intrust you with the entire direction of the missionary part of the expedition to Fuegia just commencing, and I pray God may give you wisdom, kindness, and courage from Jesus Christ for your work. I think it advisable you should proceed as rapidly as possible to Woollya, and stay there as much time as can be allowed, consistently with the return of the schooner to Stanley in time for the next mail. Should there be a very friendly spirit in Woollya I would try and spend two or three days there on shore in the house erected during my last visit there, and get a hand from the vessel to stop with you. The captain will furnish you with biscuits, &c., for encouragement to the natives, and I recommend you to cause a garden to be dug, and seeds to be sown, &c.

" Spend every day with the natives. Keep your notebook and pencil going. . . . . I look to you to undertake the services in the *Allen Gardiner*, and would advise, when

the weather allows, that you should have Sabbath morning
and evening service on shore, that the natives may attend
and be roused to inquiry.

"I have no doubt but that you and Captain Fell will,
with the blessing of God, agree well together, and that he
will render you every assistance you may reasonably require
of him. May our Lord Jesus Christ be your strength and
your shield, and bless your efforts with ample success.—
Yours, &c.   G. P. D."

After full time had been allowed for the visit, and no
signs of the returning vessel were seen from day to day, Mr
Despard became anxious for the safety of his friends, and
went to Stanley as soon as possible to take measures for
ascertaining the cause of their detention. The result was
that Captain Smyley was despatched in the schooner *Nancy*
to Woollya. The melancholy intelligence which he brought
back is thus stated by Mr Despard :—

" Mr Phillips, Captain Fell, and the four seamen and two
mates of the schooner have been massacred by the natives in
Woollya. Let me pause, and weep, and pray, now that I
have written these terrible words. Pray ye to the Lord not
to lay this sin to their charge. Weep not for the dead, weep
for the living. Weep not for the dead in Christ ; weep for
the mourning widows ; weep for the mothers deprived of
their sons, their support. God has tried us in the furnace of
affliction. May His work be perfected ! May the Lord of
the harvest send out others to supply the room of those He
has taken, and bow to contrition these poor sinners of the
Gentiles that they may be prepared for His word."

A former mate of the *Allen Gardiner* wrote to the secretary
on this occasion :—" God, for some wise purpose, permitted
me to leave the *Allen Gardiner* at the close of her last voyage,
yet I almost envy those who have been found worthy to bear

a martyr's cross, and to wear a martyr's crown. Having witnessed in the walk of Captain Fell and Mr Phillips the fruit of the Spirit, I have a confident hope that the Lord, the righteous Judge, will place the crown upon their heads."

The following is a short account of the facts. The party reached Woollya on the 1st of November, utterly unsuspicious of the catastrophe which awaited them. The opinion had gained possession of the missionary party that, degraded and ignorant as the islanders were, they were not bloodthirsty. The missionaries continued in friendly intercourse with them for several days, during which time many canoes arrived from neighbouring islands, but still nothing that occurred appears to have caused alarm, so that on Sunday the 6th, the whole ship's company, with one exception, went on shore for public worship. This was the moment chosen for an attack; a rush was made upon them, and all were barbarously murdered; not a hand was raised for their defence, but Okokko was observed by the cook, who was left on board, running up and down the beach in great distress. It seems plain that a spirit of covetousness possessed the whole multitude, and that the presence of men of another and fiercer tribe gave occasion to this sudden attack. The survivor, seeing from the deck what was going forward, escaped in a boat to the shore, hid himself in the woods till hunger and cold drove him to the natives, by the first party of whom he was stripped and plundered; but subsequently, on his return to Woollya, he was treated with uniform kindness by the Button family till the arrival of Captain Smyley in the *Nancy*. The missionary schooner had been entirely ransacked and plundered, but it was not burnt or otherwise destroyed, and was eventually conveyed, by Captain Smyley, back to the Falkland Islands and refitted.

When Captain Smyley went a second time to Woollya, for the purpose of bringing away the wreck, Okokko was so earnest in his entreaties to be taken back to his friends at Keppel, that Smyley was induced to accede to his request; and for a long time this young man and his wife Camilenna were the only Fuegian residents at the station. They proved to be most tractable and affectionate. Okokko made progress in reading and writing, besides working in the garden, and digging peat, and returned from work to find his table neatly laid and dinner prepared by Camilenna, who received daily instruction from Mrs Despard and her daughters in all sorts of housewifery, as well as reading and writing. Okokko said that Lucca and Pinoiensee wanted to come back, and that the women who had been at Keppel cried bitterly at the massacre.*

About this time Mr Despard decided on bringing his family to England: the missionary farm and property were left under the care of William Bartlett, the natives being under the charge of Mr Bridges, a young man who had been adopted and brought up by Mr Despard, and who has proved himself in every way worthy of the trust reposed in him. His duty was to continue the instruction of Okokko and Camilenna, and, in the absence of a clergyman, to conduct daily and Sunday worship.

Mr and Mrs Despard and their family arrived in England early in 1862.

* A memoir of Mr Phillips has since been published by Wertheim and Mackintosh.

CHAPTER VII.

ON the return of the *Allen Gardiner* to England, in January 1862, it was determined to add to her length, and thereby increase her efficiency as a sea boat, and the accommodation for those on board. This was accomplished; and in August of that year, with a fresh missionary party, she left Bristol for her work in the Antarctic Ocean. A favourable passage was made to the River Plate, where for three weeks the vessel remained, while Mr Stirling, the new Superintendent, visited Monte Video and Buenos Ayres in the interests of the Mission. In both these places committees were formed, and pecuniary aid was given towards the work in the south. But while attention was drawn to the special sphere of operations for which the *Allen Gardiner* was designed, and to occupy which the Mission party on board had come out, a strong and earnest desire was expressed by several persons of influence that a wider development should be given to the Society's agencies. Opportunities of Christian usefulness were pointed out on all sides, and the value of the Society as a means of turning these to good account was thoroughly recognised.

Leaving the River Plate, the *Allen Gardiner* proceeded on her voyage to the Rio Negro, which is the northern boundary of Patagonia. The visit to this place, and also to the river Santa Cruz, and the missionary work in those parts, will be

referred to in another chapter; and we mention it in passing
now, merely to account for the fact that the *Allen Gardiner*
did not reach Keppel Island in the Falklands till January
30, 1863.   There were at the mission station at this time but
two adult natives of Tierra del Fuego, and their two little children.   The prescribed course of work had been, in fact, in-
terrupted by the massacre already spoken of, and the subsequent return to England of Mr Despard and his family.
Yet the interval had not been wholly lost time.   On the contrary, Mr Bridges had diligently applied himself, under
favourable circumstances, to the acquisition of the Fuegian
language, and the moral effect on Okokko and his wife of their
sojourn at the mission station was very marked.   An extract
from Mr Stirling's journal, referring to his arrival at Keppel
Island, will not be out of place here :—

"From the water the station does not bear a very prepos-
sessing look—the houses are not grouped for effect; and,
architecturally, are not imposing.   The views from the land,
on the contrary, are full of interest.   The high lands of
the Falklands and the islands so thickly scattered, and so
richly occupied with beetling rock and pinnacle, now glow
with purple in the hazy prospect, or stand out sharp and
clear under a cloudless sky, the ever-changing sea rolling
grandly between.   On landing, we were met on the jetty by
William Bartlett and Okokko.   The latter's wife and two
children were watching us from a little distance.   The letters
announcing our approach had never reached the station, but
the possibility of such a thing did not occur to me, and I failed
to introduce myself by name until Bartlett's difficulty was
manifest on attempting to introduce me to his wife.   Okokko
surprised me by his good English, pleasant manners, and joyous
laugh.   He and his family have had many advantages since
1859 ; but if in less than four years the result of education
and kind treatment are so conspicuously good in their case

those who labour for the future benefit of these people have the utmost encouragement and rewards in store. I cannot fail to hope, moreover, that though at the present time there is much need of a deeper insight into the faith of Christ on Okokko's part than he can be said to have, (such in fact as would justify me in baptizing him,) he is, nevertheless, very capable as well as desirous of teaching his countrymen many of the lessons that he has learned, both from the word of God and the practices of Christian family life. Okokko foretells the time when, he being old and his children grown up, the whole people of Tierra del Fuego shall be taught to know God, and enjoy in peaceable habitations the fruits of Christian civilisation. This is his own picture, and the time of the prophecy his own.

"Perhaps I ought to have given an earlier place in my letter to the mention of Mr Bridges. I am satisfied that he holds in his hand, and can use far better than any one else, the key of the Fuegian language. He has caught the verbal formations, and traced them through all their intricacies. He accompanies me in the *Allen Gardiner* to Tierra del Fuego, where Okokko and his family will also go, but our stay must be short, as the season is already far advanced."

An anecdote may nelp to give an impression of the action upon Okokko's mind at this time of what he had been taught. In reply to a question by Mr Stirling, William Bartlett said— " I would rather have Okokko to work with me than half the English lads ; " and added—" He is very much changed, that he is, from what he was when he first came. Any person can see it. But he has got a quick temper." " How has he shown it ? Has he done any act of violence ?" " No, sir ; he has done no act of violence ; but the other day I went down to Mr Bridges' house, and found Okokko there in a great passion with Mr Bridges, who could do nothing with him." " And what did you do ?" " Why, sir, I told him he had better come out with me in the garden, and work a bit." "And did he come?" "He came, sir; and when he was working, I talked to him about his temper, and told him it was very wrong to be so quick angry; that Mr Bridges was his very good friend; and that God would be angry with him if he gave way to such violent temper." "What reply did he make?" "He said, in his way of speaking, ' God does not answer prayer now as He used to. Mr Bridges tells me, if I pray, God will give me a new heart, and He hasn't done it.' "

It was thus made plain to the missionary party just arrived, that they were entering upon other men's labours. Not only had a station, with all its details of farming and gardening, been formed in Keppel Island; not only had the way been pioneered; not only had the language of a Fuegian tribe been in great measure acquired; but a breaking in of light upon the mind of one at least of these natives was perceptible. It was encouraging to the new comers to find that Okokko had earned a reputation for industry, and that he had learned to pray.

Before proceeding further, it may be well to give some account of the people and country of Tierra del Fuego. We are indebted to Darwin for the following summary of its physical features and zoology:—" The country may be described as a mountainous land, partly submerged in the sea, so that deep inlets and bays occupy the place where valleys should exist. The mountain sides, except on the exposed western coast, are covered from the water's edge upwards by one great forest. The trees reach to an elevation of between 1000 and 1500 feet, and are succeeded by a band of peat, with minute Alpine plants, and this again is succeeded by the line of perpetual snow. Level land is scarcely to be found. The zoology of Tierra del Fuego is very poor. Of mammalia, besides whales and seals, there are one bat, a kind of mouse,

two true mice, two foxes, a sea-otter, the guanaco, and a deer.
Most of these animals inhabit only the drier eastern parts of
the country. The gloomy woods are inhabited by few birds.
No reptiles are found throughout the country."

To compensate for this dearth of animal life on land, the
waters of the sea are abundantly stocked with living creatures.
Darwin thus speaks of them :—

" In all parts of the world, a rocky and partially protected
shore perhaps supports in a given space a greater number of
individual animals than any other station. There is one
marine production, which, from its importance, is worthy of
a particular history. It is the kelp, or macrocystis pyrifera.
This plant grows on every rock, from low-water mark to a
great depth, both on the outer coast and within the channels.
The number of living creatures of all orders whose existence
intimately depends on the kelp is wonderful. A great volume
might be written describing the inhabitants of one of these
beds of sea-weed. I can only compare these great aquatic
forests of the southern hemisphere with the terrestrial ones in
the inter-tropical regions. Yet, if in any country a forest was
destroyed, I do not believe that nearly so many species of
animals would perish as would here from the destruction of
the kelp. Amidst the leaves of this plant, numerous species
of fish live, which nowhere else could find food or shelter.
With their destruction, the many cormorants and other fishing birds, the otters, seals, and porpoises, would soon perish
also; and lastly the Fuegian savage, the miserable lord of
this miserable land, would redouble his cannibal feasts, de-
crease in numbers, and perhaps cease to exist."

Further acquaintance with the Fuegians leads us to doubt
whether cannibalism exists at all among them. The Fuegians
may be roughly divided into canoe Indians and foot Indians,
the latter occupying the main island. The foot Indians are
a superior race to the canoe Indians, more akin to those

of Patagonia. They rarely use canoes, but live on the spoils of the chase.

The Fuegian climate is damp and windy, but equable. The mean temperature in winter and summer is about 33°. It is doubtful whether corn will ripen there; yet evergreen trees flourish, and humming-birds may be seen sucking the flowers, and parrots feeding on the seeds of the winterbark, in lat. 55 S. The southern hemisphere is occupied to a far larger extent than the northern by water, which accounts for the equable climate. The snow-line descends to 4000 or 3500 feet above the level of the sea, In the northern hemisphere, to meet with perpetual snow at this low level, we must travel to Norway between lat. 67° and 70°.

On the east coast the natives use a guanaco skin as a cloak; on the west, seal skins are used. Among the central tribes the men for the most part have either an otter skin or a seal skin as a partial protection for the body. But some are to be found entirely destitute of clothing. Their condition is miserable indeed. Polygamy exists certainly among some of the tribes, and probably among all. Among the different tribes there seems to be no government or chief. Each tribe is surrounded more or less remotely by hostile tribes, who speak different dialects; and jealousies arise and are rendered permanent by disputes about the means of subsistence. They are a thriftless people, with no domestic animals excepting dogs; not given to tilling the ground, and dependent, in the case of the canoe Indians, on fish and fungus; in that of the foot Indians, on the skilful use of the bow and arrow. The whale is a great boon to them, for they feed on the blubber, and manufacture the bones into spearheads and other instruments of hunting, and make fishing lines of plaited sinews; yet these natives could not procure a whale for themselves, but are indebted to the swordfish for harassing and driving ashore these monsters of the deep.

The kelp and the swordfish are the mainstay of Fuegian life. The Fuegian language has no written character, and the missionary, in order to be able to instruct them has in fact to become the pupil of a savage, who inadequately fulfils the duties of his new office of teacher. Few abstract terms are found in their language. No one word, so far as we know, represents *fish*. Yet the names of all the various kinds of fish existing in those waters are in common use. More than one name is used for the same thing, according as it is regarded from this or that point of view. The accidents, rather than the essence, of a thing are seized upon; and a stranger, while endeavouring to pick up the language, is often thereby perplexed. They count no higher than three. They are, moreover, without any form of worship, have no idols, and no knowledge of God. Their language is, so far as our information extends, without a word to represent the Divine Being.

It is with the fisher or canoe Indians that the missionaries hitherto have had to do, and it is plain that, in order to give scope among them for the development of Christian principles, there must be introduced along with the precepts of the gospel the elements of civilisation. This has been borne in mind in the attempts which have been made to establish a Christian mission among them, and it has been very interesting to watch the effect of these efforts in the case of Okokko's family. We now resume our narrative.

It was the duty of Mr Stirling to re-open communications with the Fuegians, for all communication between the mission station and Tierra del Fuego had ceased after the massacre in 1859. It was important that a good understanding should be established between the missionaries and the natives. On the influence of Okokko, and his efficiency as an interpreter very much depended.

The *Allen Gardiner* sailed for Tierra del Fuego in March

1863, touching at Banner Cove, Packsaddle Bay, and Woollya.

Among those on board was Okokko. How he acquitted himself as a friend and as an interpreter will be seen by reference to extracts from Mr Stirling's journal. At Packsaddle Bay a footing of confidence was speedily established through the friendly explanations of Okokko with the family of a man named Chingaline, whose son is now in England.

"Having overheard us singing at our morning prayer, they wished us to sing again, which we did, Okokko once leading, and then Mr Bridges; and subsequently, on the shore when we landed, the man and his eldest son sat and listened with the most evident pleasure while we sang 'Praise God from whom all blessings flow,' and 'From Greenland's Icy Mountains.' I desired Okokko and Mr Bridges to make plain to this man the nature of our work, and our desire to teach and benefit his people. To this he attentively listened, and when we asked him if he would like his son to visit Keppel Island to be instructed, he was not long in talking to his boy about it before he gave his consent. The boy, too, was well pleased. And now a word about the lad, whose age is perhaps fourteen, and his name Uroopatoosaloom. In height he is just over five feet, with black hair and full laughing eyes, a very pleasant expression, good features, and a mouth just large enough to display an enviable set of white teeth. Full of gentleness and good nature is this Fuegian lad, as far removed from a savage as I am. Not a man in the *Allen Gardiner* but likes him, not a man but has expressed surprise at his good qualities, his docility, his willingness to oblige, his quick accommodation to his new circumstances, his good looks, and cleanly habits. The fact is, I went to Tierra del Fuego screwed tight up in my prejudices, and desiring to exercise a very large charity towards a people belonging to the lowest portion of the human race. To my surprise I found myself wondering at the evident resemblance to myself which these savages presented, and then unconsciously striving to convince myself that they must be worse than they seemed to be. But I think I have learnt that it is more becoming to think and speak of these people respectfully, and to observe the apostolic precept, 'Honour all men.'

"The father's last words to his son were an exhortation that he should not go ashore at Woollya, but remain in the vessel, as the natives there were not friendly with his people."

No more satisfactory evidence of confidence could be given than this. The father would trust his son to strangers, whose motives and purposes he recognised to be good, to be taken to the Falkland Islands, while yet he mistrusted his own countrymen, belonging to a neighbouring clan, distant but twenty miles. Thus was the way smoothed for a development of the plans of the Mission. The lad here referred to is one of the four who arrived in England in August 1865. We resume the journal:—

" *Woollya, March* 28.—It was very interesting to watch Okokko as he sought to impress his people with our desire to benefit them, to raise them out of their present poverty, and to teach them about God and Jesus Christ. The tone of his voice, as he addressed them, was unaffectedly earnest; and many attentive eyes and ears were fixed upon him and occupied with his words, as he spoke with an energy and animation congenial to the Fuegian mind, from the deck of the *Allen Gardiner*, to the assembled natives in the canoes about the ship. This was the first time that anything like preaching in their own tongue, and in their own land, had been addressed to these neglected people, and it seemed like the beginning of better things. It is certainly significant of a blessing on the past labours of the Mission, and prophetic, I trust, of greater blessings to come.

" *Sunday, March* 29.—He went on shore with his wife

and family, and spent the day, as he assures me, and I
have no doubt of it, in seeking to make his countrymen understand our real object, and to secure their friendly disposition towards us; telling them that the ship was built and
sent out expressly for them that they might be made acquainted with God, and know about Jesus Christ who died
for them; and that good men go to heaven, and bad men go
to hell; that if they were good we would come and teach
them many things that would profit them now, and that by
and by they should have goats, and sheep, and gardens, the
same as at Keppel Island. This is a faithful summary of
what he stated that he said to his people, as he visited them
in their wigwams; and if I may judge of the effect of his
words by the subsequent quiet and exemplary conduct of the
natives, I should say it was eminently beneficial."

Our readers will not misunderstand, or give an exaggerated
force to the word "preaching," in the foregoing extract.
They will bear in mind the very imperfectly informed state
of mind of the native who addressed his people, and the in-
capability of the people at this time of taking in the meaning of such words as God and Jesus Christ, as heaven and
hell; and the chief effect, therefore, of Okokko's address to
his countrymen must have been derived from the earnestness
of his manner, and the assurance which he gave of a friendly
spirit on the part of the missionaries. They had come "not
to destroy men's lives, but to save them."

"During the remainder of our stay at Woollya we continued on the most friendly terms with the natives. Mr
Bridges gained much *éclat* by his acquaintance with their
language, and there can be no doubt that his whole heart is
in his work."

The number of Fuegians who were desirous of visiting the
mission station were more than could be accommodated there.
But on the return of the *Allen Gardiner* to Keppel, Mr Stir-

H

·ling writes :—"We have now, with Okokko and his family, eleven natives of Tierra del Fuego under our training and care."

Shortly afterwards three Patagonians, from Santa Cruz, came in the *Allen Gardiner* to the mission station on Keppel Island. The trio were composed of a man aged about sixty, his daughter and son. In appearance they far excelled the natives of the Fuegian Archipelago, and although good-humoured and civil, they did not affect to disguise the superiority of which they were conscious. The orderly arrangements of everything at the station did not fail to strike the new comers. Nothing could be more different from all they had been accustomed to than the circumstances of their new position. The regularity of the hours of labour, of meals, and of the issuing of stores; the morning and evening services of religion to which they were summoned by the sound of the bell; the appointed periods of instruction; the attention bestowed upon the gardens and the farm; the tameness of the animals about the station; the novelties of diet, and the large use of vegetables; the contrasts between the toldo, or the wigwam, and the snug cottage; the differences of clothing, and the importance attached to cleanliness in every particular; these, and a hundred other matters utterly beyond the range of their past experience—in themselves so small as almost to escape our notice—immediately arrested the observation of these strangers, and exercised a wonderful influence upon their imaginations. The new life was a series of surprises to them. Yet they fell in with its requirements easily; and the occasions on which it was necessary to enforce a rule, when once understood, were remarkably rare.

But with all its novelties and restrictions, Keppel Island was well adapted as a place of training for the natives. The climate is healthy and invigorating, rendering bodily exercise pleasant. The daily necessities of supplying food and

fuel by steady industry in the extensive mission gardens and
the peat valley, or by the more exciting pursuit of the cattle,
now running wild in the camp, harmonised at once the aims
of the missionaries with the instincts of the natives. In the
gardens were laid the foundation of orderly habits of labour,
while expeditions into the camp for beef, relieved the insular
life of its monotony, by satisfying that innate love of the
chase, which is so strong a passion in the South American
races. As a consequence, the natives were generally healthy;
and, not being afflicted with "long thinking," accepted with
great readiness the new conditions of life in which they were
placed. In the morning they regularly attended the services,
which commenced the day; attentive and reverent in their
manner, not indeed at first understanding all that took
place, but imbued with the solemnity of the proceedings, and
carrying away with them convictions of a worship due to the
unseen Spirit. The morning service over, lessons commenced.
In one class are the little boys—it may be, just arrived from
their own country. They know but a few stray words of
English, and their own language offers no means of telling
them about God, and of the gift of His Son, and of His kingdom. Words to express these things, even in a mutilated
form, are wanting in their tongue. The basis of Christian
instruction must be the English language. Accordingly, by
line upon line, precept upon precept, here a little and there
a little, the young lads are familiarised with Christian truths
in English, and their memories are exercised by verses of
Scripture, or hymns, which they are taught to repeat. At
first, the process of instruction is to them an amusing puzzle,
and there are frequent smiles on the part of some who
possess a more facile utterance than their companions, at
false pronunciations made by them. One remarks, to the
evident satisfaction of the majority, that so and so, in his
attempts at English, "*brays* like a penguin." The allusion is

not polite, but exceedingly good-humoured, and nobody is offended. A laugh of approval is the only consequence. By degrees the bearing upon their daily life of what they have been committing to memory begins to strike them. The God about whom they have lately heard for the first time is He, in obedience to whose commands the missionaries are there to teach them, is the One whose law Englishmen acknowledge, is a God of mercy, desirous of doing good, not evil to men—is the Maker of all things, knows all things, sees all things, governs all things. Thus far, it may be said, the natives, under regular instruction, show a readiness to accept what is taught. They listen, too, with satisfaction to the evidence of God's love in the gift of His Son; but the Atonement has its manifest difficulties to their minds, and it may be questioned whether this fundamental truth has hitherto been truly received in its fulness by any of the natives. As a statement of fact, they believe it; but, from the absence of deep sin-conviction, they have not yet learned the value of that blood shed for the forgiveness of sin. Their outward conduct, however, answers rapidly to the new principle of action which the gospel enforces; and lads from Tierra del Fuego, belonging to the degraded tribes of that benighted land, show, in their general demeanour and docility, how capable they are of profiting by the instruction given.

The more advanced youths are meanwhile pursuing their studies, slowly indeed, but satisfactorily,—here engaged in learning to write and there in reading, while all are taught some text of Scripture, on which they will be presently questioned. The hours of morning school are not long. At 11 A.M. they are expected to be at their outdoor work, and not till the evening will they again be in the presence of the black-board and their primers, or storing their minds with some lines of a hymn, which on the morrow they will sing

together.   It is a happy thing that these natives are musical,
for the hymns and chants in the Church services delight
them, and very pleasant it is to hear their young voices singing, in sweet accord, words and tunes familiar to our English
ears.

We have spoken of our male pupils.   Girls are not visitors
at our station.   Only married women are invited; nor
would others be permitted by the natives of Tierra del
Fuego to come under our care.   These are few in number,
and have scarcely received such regular instruction as their
husbands and the boys have enjoyed.   Still they have profited to a considerable degree by their sojourn on Keppel
Island, and have, in acquiring the habits of civilised life, prepared themselves for future usefulness.   The wife of Okokko,
owing to the early training received from Mr Despard's family,
and followed up by others, is as capable of keeping house
and looking after her children, their clothes, &c., and making
a home for her husband, as most English labourers' wives.
Her knowledge of English, and facility of reading and writing, are at least on a par with Okokko's; and all that we can
desire for her is the fulness of the Divine grace, which alone
sanctifies and transforms the human heart.   Of the other
women we can speak hopefully.   They interest and encourage in many ways those who seek their good, but it would be
wrong to say more than this, and allow mere wishes to out-
strip one's judgment.

It may be suggested that the comforts and regularity of
life on Keppel Island unfit, to some extent, those who have
enjoyed them, for the ruder state of things in their own home,
and that the natives thus trained are thereby more or less separated, in feeling and interest, from their fellow-countrymen.
Without denying that there is some truth in this, it is yet
satisfactory to know that the natural affection of these
natives for their people is a pretty safe counteracting influence

to danger of this kind. We find, for instance, Okokko, after a protracted stay at the mission station, expressing his desire to settle amongst his people, lest by a too long separation he should lose his influence for good over them. At a time when this man and his family were the only ones properly prepared to set an example of Christian civilisation in Tierra del Fuego, he courageously preferred settling there to waiting till others might be more advanced, and ready to aid him in his enterprise. It is true certain natives who had been on Keppel Island belonged to his tribe, and were living in his neighbourhood, and even promised to aid him; but they were young, and, as it proved, without influence, and only most imperfectly instructed. This fact speaks much in favour of the system adopted by the Society. We now revert to Mr Stirling's journal, which gives an account of the voyage to Tierra del Fuego, and the establishment at Woollya of Okokko and his family. The date is Woollya:—

"On February 18, 1864, the *Allen Gardiner* left Keppel for Woollya. Okokko was now about to settle in Tierra del Fuego, and there to create a home. Camilenna, his wife, was no longer to fish and wander in the canoe. Her position for the future was to resemble that of an English wife; she was to stay at home, take care of the children, and present to her people an example of domestic life. I give you the idea of Okokko—not mine, or any one else's—respecting his wife's future mode of life in her own country. As for the other Fuegians, all was cheerfulness and mirth; one might think they were returning to some cheerful, well-appointed home, and not to the rude privileges of the wigwam and the bark canoe. But, in fact, it was the joyousness of youth and health, the flush of pleasure which 'packing-up and going away' produces in boys, or the love of change so deep in young hearts, that caused such unwonted animation in the *Allen Gardiner*.

" On the 27th the anchor was let go in Lennox Cove. We had our first interview with the natives at Gretton Bay, Wollaston Island. On arriving at Packsaddle Bay, a gloom was cast over the minds of the natives on board by rumours of a fatal malady which, in the past summer, had carried off large numbers of the people. Every one of our party was said to have lost relations. T. Button had lost two brothers; Threeboys his father, and other relations. All Camilenna's relations had died ; and Lucca, too, had lost uncles and cousins; Uroopa's father had become a widower, &c. An unaffected grief took possession of our lately happy company of natives: the saddest of all, perhaps, was Threeboys, whose father, James Button, was now reported to be dead. Poor Camilenna, too, had one long night of weeping, and Okokko's eyes in the morning looked swollen and heavy. Tom Button came to me more than once, saying, 'Mr Stirling, I very unhappy; by and by happy,' and his face bore traces of a saddened spirit. We were requested not to allude to the deceased by name, for the Fuegians, like the Patagonians, and other Indians, bury in silence the names of the departed. Our sympathy was expressed in words of kindness ; but I longed for a larger utterance of the love and life which are in Christ to cheer and quicken the mourners' hearts. A desire to proceed quickly to Woollya was, of course, the result of the above intelligence, and on Monday, the wind being fair, the captain got the vessel under way. Uroopa's father, who belongs to this neighbourhood, was absent; the weather had been adverse to his coming; but, in fact, the canoe party, who undertook to fetch him, never fulfilled their contract, and Chingaline was not aware of the *Allen Gardiner's* presence with his son on board. On March the 7th we reached Woollya. On our passage thither we saw several canoes in snug corners, some moored to the kelp, and the natives in them fishing, some paddling along in shore, while one more bold than the rest attempted to intercept us, and a voice, as we hastened by—(the captain letting the ship go off a little, to avoid running the canoe down)—remonstrated with us for not taking the venturesome craft in tow. It was dark, and a drizzling rain falling, when we anchored in Woollya. The approach of the vessel was the signal for a burst of mournful news; and loud and melancholy sounded the tidings of death. There had been a malignant sickness, and old and young, very many, had been swept away by it. James Button was dead.

"On the following morning we were early visited by the people, but their number was not large. As the day advanced, however, canoes kept coming in, yet not numerously, as a fresh breeze agitated the waters in the Sound too much to allow canoes comfortably to cross it. On the third, or fourth day, the entire Woollya party had probably assembled, and forty canoes were reckoned at one time in the harbour. Poor Jamesina, as Mr Despard used to call James Button's wife, visited the ship the day after its arrival, and in her canoe were eleven persons, mostly young. Her face was full of sorrow; and, pointing with her finger toward the sky, she gave me to understand, by looks more than words, the cause of her grief, and how great it was. A majority of the natives had the hair cut short on the crown of the head, and other evidences of mourning were frequent. Our presence among them, however, produced daily a more cheerful tone.

"We miss many once familiar faces. It is remarkable that the sickness of which I have spoken should not have occurred until after the return of the *Allen Gardiner*, subsequently to the massacre, and as a pledge of the forgiveness of their enemies which Christians can show; but there are so many suggestive providences in the history of our Mission, that to dwell on them would destroy the character of this letter as a chronicle of facts. I therefore forbear.

"On March 7th, the boat is manned at 9.45 A.M., and,

ander the command of the captain, proceeds to Button Island. Mr Bridges accompanies me in the boat. Okokko and Pinoiensee guide us into a pleasant cove, which they consider suitable for their future dwelling. A site for a station is the object of our search. The water is deep up to the landing-place; in the kelp close by, an old sea-lion was just now sleeping; a young fur-seal every now and then poked his head above water, but took no pains to wake the drowsy lion. Startled by a bullet from our boat, the huge creature has leaped bodily into the air, and with a fierce plunge disappeared beneath the deep waters. That seal would have been a prize for their people, but they still hope that some fortunate canoe party may fall in with and secure it. On landing, we cannot but admire the spot, and the scarlet flower of the mugoo, (Fuegian name,) a beautiful shrub, shines out with dazzling brilliancy. There is a narrow valley before us, but it looks as if winter floods chased down it. The rocks rise precipitous to the right and left, with a gorge here and there, up which the thin verdure slopes in a feigned fertility. The soil is good beneath our feet, and Okokko praises it highly. The grass grows luxuriantly, and the wild currant too: but the space available for the purposes of a settlement admits of very narrow development, and it is resolved that we examine another locality.

" A row of two miles or so brings us to a spot very superior in every respect to the one just visited. There is abundance of good ground, good wood, good water, good grass. A walk on shore well repays us, by its frequent introduction to something new and interesting. Here is the funeral pyre on which the body of one of Macooallan's brothers was recently burned—here the wigwam or framework of branches, where for a day the body lay in state. The body of James Button has not yet been burned; it is merely interred. The return of his brother from Keppel Island has been waited for, and now the remains will be submitted to the flames. This information is given to us in a subdued voice by Okokko. Half a mile from where we leave the boat there is a lake. It is muffled round with woods, through which we have approached it. From the trees the boys have gathered two kinds of fungus, which we taste, and while tasting, think the natives not so badly off after all. I may here say that there are some twenty different sorts of fungus, and these come in distinct seasons, so that for several months in the year at least food of that kind is plentiful. Berries, too, in summer are abundant, and of various kinds. In fact, whilst staying at Woollya, it is an almost daily matter to see files of men and boys returning from the woods, laden with these fruits of the season. We retrace our steps to the landing-place, thinking we can do no better than determine on this place for the establishment of Okokko. But down that rugged steep, the captain says, comes the fitful hurricane, the 'Williwaw;' and he dislikes the place for anchorage, with its deep waters and possible blasts. We begin to fear lest the proper safeguards for the ship may be compromised if we cling to our land projects; for to anchor for a night or two is one thing—to anchor off the place, while a station is being laid out on shore, is altogether another. However, here is a breeze, and the boat-sail is hoisted, and we are hastening back to our little vessel at Woollya, thinking a decked-boat would be much safer in these windy channels, and putting off a decision as to the place of Okokko's settlement. The ship is reached by 3.30 P.M., and the chief officer reports favourably of the conduct of the natives during the day. In the evening, Mr Rau tells me that Lucca has pointed out the exact spot where were placed the dead bodies of our friends who fell in Nov. 1859. It is not two hundred yards from where the *Allen Gardiner* lies at anchor. The next morning I question Lucca about it, and he speaks confidently on the subject. He helped to convey one body to the spot in question, and he and Okokko covered the bodies with large stones, lest the foxes should devour them. Okokko corroborates all this. At once the boat is lowered, and we proceed to the place. Great fragments of rock lie here one upon another, the lowest washed by the waters of the bay, the highest about eighteen feet above them. Overhanging all is the solid rock, rising with a bold front some thirty feet, and then falling back under cover of the descending forest. We scramble over the broken rocks, and presently traces of the deceased come to light. The remains of Mr Phillips and Captain Fell are unmistakable, and I have no doubt that six of the bodies of our beloved friends were placed entire where we sought them, that they were placed there in their clothes, and that not even their pockets were rifled.

"In the afternoon of the 11th of March I read the funeral service, partly in the ship, and partly by the grave. For the Collect immediately succeeding the Lord's Prayer, I substituted that for St Stephen's Day; otherwise, I adhered to the accustomed English service. The flag hung half-mast high, and every token of reverent feeling was unaffectedly offered. The hymn beginning

> "'When our heads are bow'd with woe,
> When our bitter tears o'erflow,
> When we mourn the lost, the dear,
> Jesu, born of woman, hear,'

concluded the solemn service, and the booming of the ship's two signal guns announced aloud that it was over."

It was a coincidence not overlooked that, on the very day on which the remains of the party massacred were discovered, the chapter read at the evening service on board the *Allen Gardiner*, and coming in the ordinary course, was Isaiah xxv. Those present had their attention directed to the remarkable promise,—" And He will destroy in this mountain the face of the covering cast over all people, and the veil that is spread over all nations. He will swallow up death in victory, and the Lord God will wipe away tears from off all faces; and the rebuke of His people shall He take away from off all the earth, for the Lord hath spoken it."

The physical aspects of the place corresponded with the language of the prophet, and the taking away of the veil cast over all people, and the victory over death, and the wiping away of tears, foretold and secured by the mouth of the Lord, seemed to fit in and harmonise with the circumstances of the work, and the earnest longings of those engaged in it.

" On the 11th of March, Macooallan (i.e., T. Button) ventured to resume life in the wigwam. His wife and two children accompanied him, also Pinoiensee. We gave him some biscuit, and rice, and beans, with about six lbs. of sugar. He expressed himself as pleased with our kindness. Now, I should like to say something of this man, but how to do so without danger of saying too much, or too little, I do not know. You will, however, understand that he is in a very inferior degree, so far as I can see, inwardly acquainted with Christian truth. His mind is, I fear, very dark Sometimes I am told he gives vent to the expression, ' What will become of me ?' in a tone suggestive of earnest, though perplexed inquiry. His manner, too, is reverent, and has a semblance of intelligence in our public worship. Privately he listens with apparent interest to a chapter of the Bible, or some oral statement of truth; but he cannot read, and when not actually within the living zone of Christian influence, and left to stand alone without the direct guidance of Christian teachers, there is, perhaps, little reason to expect from him more than a general improvement in manners. Mr Rau, however, and I rejoice to say it, cherishes a far more hopeful view of Macooallan's state of mind. At Keppel Island he formed no steady habit of industry, although he was ever ready to serve me, and at times gave voluntary assistance in the gardens, &c. His age cannot be less than fifty, I think; and at that time of life old habits are difficult to be broken up. Yet I look for some positive advantages to the Mission work from his influence amongst his country people, and from the gentle temper and grateful spirit of his wife.

"It is finally determined, after examination of several neighbouring islets, to erect a dwelling and goat-house for Okokko, at Woollya, close to the spot where the dilapidated hut stands.

"On Monday morning, the 14th inst., Chingaline arrived at Woollya. He has heard of our recent visit in Packsaddle Bay, and of our present whereabouts, so he has come to see his son. In the canoe with him are two young women, sisters, (one married, the other single,) a strong and active looking young man, (the husband of the married woman,) and a brother of Uroopa, aged, perhaps, nine years. Not one of the new comers ventures to land; for friendly relations between the people of Packsaddle Bay and Woollya are not reliable. But the deck of the *Allen Gardiner* is neutral ground, and there Chingaline and his nephew, the man just spoken of, delight to stand. We give them a hospitable reception, and beyond all doubt a good measure of satisfaction is experienced by our visitors, by Chingaline most particularly, who finds his son so strong and well, and contented with his lot. The father wishes Uroopa to go with him in the canoe, to which we immediately agree, and presently— his box being brought up, and all his little property handed down into the canoe—we say good-bye to, and follow with many good wishes, a lad who has won, and kept to the last, the affection of us all. Threeboys came to me, and in a tone. of real sorrow inquired if Uroopa was not coming back. 'Uroopa, a nice boy, I plenty like Uroopa. He not come back?' and then he added, ' perhaps ship go again to Packsaddle?' Lucca no less earnestly expressed his regret at Uroopa's departure, and declared his hearty friendship towards him. But all that day somebody was missed on board the *Allen Gardiner*.

" Lucca's determination is to return to Keppel Island. Threeboys also, who contemplated residence in Tierra del Fuego, has requested leave to remain with us since the death of his father has been ascertained. Petitions to go to Keppel Island are daily urged. The *Allen Gardiner* could never carry all who would like to come. The difficulty is to make a selection. But I am desirous to take to our station for instruction one little fellow, a cousin of Threeboys, whose small confidences reposed in me have quite won my heart. He seems to pick up English by instinct; he has a twink-ling eye and knowing look, but, above all, he is of a gentle and confiding nature, and most pliable age. When I am on shore, he is seldom far from me, and evidences his attach-ment by inviting me to sit down to a fungus repast with him. He is an orphan. In the late sickly season his father suc-cumbed to the prevailing epidemic; the little boy, too, suf-fered from the sickness, as his attenuated limbs testify, but God has raised him up to be a monument perhaps of His highest mercies. To come to Keppel Island is his great desire. The people generally hold him in much affection, and will not let him go without the boy making plain his own wish on the subject. I go on one occasion into the woods, seeking a quiet place, apart from the crowd, to read for a short time. My young ally soon finds me out, and then seating himself as close as possible by my side, begins to talk. Looking into my face with a look that would fain penetrate my inmost thoughts, he asks if I will be his good friend? I assure him I will, and he with evident pleasure states that he will ' be with ' me. (The ' be with ' is, Mr

Bridges tells me, equivalent to the same term, when we say that we throw in our lot with any one.) So I find there is at least one young heart in Tierra del Fuego, which confides in me, and wishes to join its lot to mine. Keppel Island then became a subject of conversation, and I soon found out what a diligent gleaner of news my companion was. He had stored his mind with the whole vocabulary of civilisation at our station. 'Keppel Island, horse, cow, sheep, goat, spoon, pannikin, pig, towel, soap, potatoes, turnips, &c.' When he came to the pig I was greatly amused, for I had not seen one for a long time, and it seemed to me to be a new piece of information that I was picking up; but on the island, of course, there are pigs, and my intelligent friend was quite right. As he thoughtfully, and without the remotest suggestion from me, enumerated the various things belonging to the station, I was not a little surprised; for the boy is small enough to be seven years old only, although he may be more. I wish to take *him* to Keppel Island. The children generally I encourage to approach me; and with the help of Threeboys as interpreter, who has marched at the head of a file of children to the old hut, which I had appointed as a schoolroom for the occasion, I form a class of scholars.

" On Friday, March 18, our visitors to Keppel Island were finally assorted. An assembly had the day before been made of those most desirous of going with us, and out of these I selected eight. Lucca and Threeboys are exclusive of this number. Okokko is now in possession of a house built for him.

" On Saturday nothing worthy of notice occurred. We visit Okokko in his new dwelling, and find him occupied in cooking fish for the family breakfast. He seemed in good spirits. Stores were left by us for his use during the next seven months, at the end of which period I expect to be with him again. Without some such supplies, both Okokko and

his wife would be thrown back upon canoe life, to the neglect
of the children, of the projected gardens, and all that concerns
the future introduction of civilised manners.   As it is, they
will now have sufficient stores to enable them with care to
pass the coming winter without suffering, while Okokko's
time can be principally devoted to the preparation of ground
for a garden, fencing it in, attending to his goats, improving
his house, and covering it with bark, when the season for
procuring bark arrives.   Nevertheless, it will be quite necessary for him to depend to a large extent on fish, and mussels,
and the edible fungi, to which the stores left with him are
after all but supplementary.

" Sunday, the 20th, is a quiet day with us, the natives
paying marked regard to our observance of it.   In the afternoon many canoes leave the bay, and I go ashore to visit
Okokko, who has not been present at our service in the ship.
He could not well leave his house, he said, but he had had
prayer at home.   His prayer-book he took immediately from
his pocket, and when he had sung, ' I will arise and go to
my father,' I asked him to read the Collect for the day,
which he did, and which formed a basis of my parting exhortation to him.   As I was saying good-bye he asked me,
in a simple, earnest manner, to pray for him when I was
away.

" Our visit at Woollya closed on the morning of the 21st.
We have been remarkably favoured by the weather; the
natives, too, have been quiet and friendly in their conduct to
us.   We have had the satisfaction of interring the long-lost
remains of our predecessors in the missionary work ; we
have, by word and act, endeavoured to set forth the mercies
of God and the grace of Jesus Christ; we have been permitted to lay the foundations, as we hope, of a Christian
civilisation in these hitherto savage parts; and, notwithstanding the apparently small beginning, we have, as our

knowledge of the work to be done increases, an increasing hopefulness of its ultimate success."

It was a matter of encouragement that Okokko was not only in possession of a prayer-book in the phonetic character, but able to use it, and aware of its value. "Mr Stirling, will you pray for me?" were likewise encouraging words at this time, especially coming from the lips of one who, a few months before, had said, "God does not answer prayer now." The ship sailed with her party of natives for the mission station, and Okokko was left to stand his ground almost alone. How did he conduct himself? and did he seek at all to instruct his people? We give the following testimony. "Okokko," said one of the natives of Woollya, referring subsequently to this subject, "had often spoken to the people of God, of heaven, and hell, and what sort of people should live in them. His people being very proud, and bad, would not listen, and were sometimes very angry, and said Okokko told lies; that as they had never seen nor heard God, they would not believe him, and that man, and all things had ever been as they are, without beginning, and therefore without a Maker. One man pretended to be Jesus Christ. Some were afraid to be in hell, and wished to become quiet, as a requisite preparation for heaven: some threatened to kill Okokko, but were afraid to do so." During Okokko's stay on this occasion, and in his new circumstances, at Woollya, gardens were laid out and fenced in, and sown with potatoes and turnips. A serviceable bridge, across a neighbouring stream, indicated a desire to extend improvement, and the goats were carefully tended. The original flock of seven had increased to upwards of twenty. A commencement had been made of civilisation; a witness for the truth had been planted in Tierra del Fuego. It was but a feeble beginning, what was to be its issue?

When the *Allen Gardiner* visited Woollya, in March 1865,

I

it was found, to the great regret of all, that Okokko's house, and goats, and property, had been destroyed by fire. A fit of jealousy, and some pretence of the invasion of tribal rights in occupying the particular spot where the house and garden were established, had caused three natives, when Okokko and his friends were absent on a fishing expedition, to destroy all his property.

When Okokko came on board the Mission schooner he showed signs of great distress at what had happened, and especially lamented that in the conflagration he had lost his Bible and prayer-book. The genuineness of this regret there is no reason to doubt. He knew the difficulty of replacing them, as they were printed in the phonetic character, which alone he could read, and there were no similar copies at the station. The ordinary Roman type was to him utterly strange.

In consequence of this untoward event, it was determined that Okokko and his family should return once more to the mission station on Keppel Island, along with other natives, for further instruction, and with a view to prepare a better organised party for location in Tierra del Fuego. This was the more expedient, as the *Allen Gardiner* was about to return to England, with Mr Stirling on board, and it would, in all probability, be a considerable time before another visit to Woollya could be paid. To have left Okokko there with impoverished resources, and for a longer time than usual, would have been unwise. His determination to follow up a course of Christian civilisation, in his own country, was in no degree weakened by what had occurred. All he desired were the means to do it.

The *Allen Gardiner* returned to the Falklands with the Fuegians on board in April, and, besides Okokko and his family, Lucca and Pinoiensee and their wives, and two other lads, Tirshof and Yesefwaenges were left at the mission station, under the care and instruction of Mr Bridges. Four others accompanied Mr Stirling to England, where they arrived in August 1865. Their names are Threeboys, Uroopa, Jack, and Sisoy or Sisoyenges. Of these the first was for some months under the instruction of Mr Despard and Mr Phillips, having gone to Keppel with his father and Mr Allen Gardiner in 1858. Uroopa went there for the first time in 1863; and the other two boys first came under instruction in 1864.

On their arrival in England these four boys remained for a short time at Bristol, under careful superintendence; but during the present year they have been placed under the care of Mr Heather, at Clarborough, near Retford. They can read the English Testament tolerably, can write fairly in a copybook, can mend their clothes, can attend to cattle, and can farm and garden in a small way. They are very attentive and orderly in the family with whom they reside. They give indications of considerable moral power. They never pass a day without private prayer; and instances have occurred of their turning to prayer as their only resource when conscious of a fault. They have attended a Bible class, without showing any inferiority to the English boys who belong to the same class: but when clergymen, who are not constantly with them, question them on scriptural subjects the Fuegians do not readily understand the drift of the questions. The reason is obvious, and if the questioner were himself questioned in a language of which he had as imperfect a knowledge as the Fuegian boys have of English, he would at once appreciate the difficulty in which they are placed. It could easily, however, be shown that they understand more of what is said to them, or in their presence, than they can express in English. Our knowledge of their language being less than their knowledge of ours, it is difficult to say more with accuracy. But we insert the testimony of the Bishop of Cork, with respect to one of them, who was present at a public meeting in Cork, at which the bishop presided. The lad was asked to speak a few words in his own tongue, to sing a portion of a hymn, and to repeat the Lord's Prayer. It was in reference to this that the bishop closed the meeting with the following remarks :—" My own conviction and persuasion is, that the most convincing address which I have heard, and the most persuasive address, and the address I shall longest remember, and the address I shall longest appreciate, was the address written upon the form and the face of the youth, and expressed in the tone of his voice; there was a softness and a sweetness in it, and a ring in it of the same quality as our own, and indicating that he is capable of attaining to our intellectuality, to our morality, our virtue. He can become, and such as he will become, an heir of God and joint-heir with Christ. I hope we shall take a deep interest in that country."

If we can thus look with satisfaction upon these youths now in England, there is likewise much to encourage us, if we look to what is going on, quietly and unobtrusively, on Keppel Island. The accounts from thence are, we think, very satisfactory, and the following portion of Mr Bridges' journal cannot fail to be read with great interest :—

" Evening prayers and Sunday afternoon instruction (in Fuegian) are regularly conducted and attended. I have gone through, since the ship's departure, the Gospels of St Matthew and St Mark, and have begun St Luke's. They were much interested in the miracles of Jesus, and in His death, resurrection, and ascension; and I have every reason to think that the lessons derived from these truths were not 'seed by the wayside' to these people. Okokko has asked many questions, and has shown great concern to be satisfied of the truth of the facts he hears stated, as though he felt their consequences. He should be particularly remembered at the Throne of Grace. This morning, after prayers, he asked me many questions, which show he takes a personal interest in what he hears. With an evident desire to do what is right, he asks me how he should act under such and such circumstances. He asked whether I were certain that Jesus rose from the dead, evidently considering this point, if established, a seal to the truth of all the rest that he had heard. He asked whether I was certain Jesus would return to the earth to make the good happy, and the wicked miserable. I unhesitatingly answered, ' Yes. He rose from the dead, on the third day of his death, and as He has said, He will most certainly return to judge the world.' He then asked whether if he repented, and asked Jesus to forgive him, and to be his friend, and save him, I was sure He would hear and grant it. I answered, ' Yes, certainly He will; that since He came into the world to die for us, and has pleased God in our stead by keeping His commandments, if we ask Him, He will most willingly grant us all we ask.' He appeared to receive heartily all I said, as of the greatest importance. He then asked me, if he should ask God to make him good, peaceable, and wise, whether He would surely hear him; and if a person should quarrel with him, how he should act. If his brother should be killed by a man how he should act. I answered these questions as I best could. He then asked me to tell Lucca, Pinoiensee, Threeboys, and Uroopa, to help him to teach his people, who, if only he taught them the truths he has learnt. would despise what he said, and despise him, as they did before.

" *Friday, Jan.* 12, 1866.—He frankly acknowledged he had a bad temper, being passionate, and he lamented that he quarrelled so much with the other natives, and he wished to be reconciled to Tirshof, and asked him to forgive him for some quarrel he had needlessly with him some time since. This may give you some idea of his state, and doubtless with me you will say, and rejoice, that this man is not far from the kingdom of heaven. He asked me to write out some prayers for him in his own language, that he might use them. He prays to God generally every evening, and often of mornings. I am much more satisfied with his character than I was, and think him much more capable to hold his ground among his people than he was.

" *Thursday, Jan.* 25.—After evening prayers I spoke to the natives, to induce them to live in love with one another. I told them plainly that if we forgive not men their trespasses neither will our heavenly Father forgive us our trespasses. I showed them that heaven was a place where all is love, and we must here become fit by the renewing of our hearts by the Holy Spirit, else we could never enter therein. Okokko and Lucca being at variance, I asked Okokko to tell us what he had said or done to raise this quarrel? He then frankly told·us. He said he was made angry in the morning by finding ashes emptied on the path, and he spoke loudly to his wife, (with intention for his next door neighbour to hear,) asking her who had done it. He then accosted Lucca. Lucca explained how it happened, but did not offer to take them up again. They then had angry words together. I told them how sad it was to me, and to all who loved them, to see and hear how ready they are to dispute. I showed them that they never could be happy, good, and prosperous, if they did not learn to forgive and love one another. We then prayed together."

Let us sum up the results of the work in Tierra del Fuego. First, a wholly new, difficult, and barbarous language has been to a great extent acquired and reduced to writing, and inlaid with words containing Christian truth. It is thus rendered capable of use as a means of daily instruction at the mission station for the natives who speak it. Secondly, the minds and hearts of several of these natives have been brought under the influence of Christian doctrine and practice. Thirdly,

they have acquired habits of industry, and learned the value
of agriculture. Fourthly, there are natives anxious to repro-
duce what they have learned amongst their countrymen in
their own land. In these things surely we may find great
encouragement. We look forward hopefully and confidently
to a Christian Church being formed in Tierra del Fuego
itself. That the Lord will bless the work of His servants we
cannot doubt. There will be a monument of grace in those
far-off islands of the sea, and a glorious memorial of the faith
and patience, the fortitude and peace, which distinguished
·the noble Gardiner and his companions who perished there.

While this book is passing through the press, the *Allen
Gardiner* is again advertised to sail for the Falklands. The
four Fuegian youths, who have, we think, benefited much
during their stay in England, and have gained many friends
through their consistent conduct, return in her to the mission
station on Keppel Island.

CHAPTER VIII.

WHILE the station on Keppel Island was being formed, with a view to sustained missionary effort among the islands of Tierra del Fuego, voyages were also made to the coast of Patagonia every year. The wandering habits of the Patagonian tribes, however, rendered visits to their coast very unsatisfactory. Plans were suggested for forming a station on the Rio Negro, and for acting from that station as a basis; but, as it was clear that means were not at the time forthcoming for carrying this out, Mr Schmid volunteered to go alone, and travel with some one of the Patagonian tribes, hoping that in this way something might be done towards acquiring the Patagonian language, or at least that a beginning of friendly communications might be made.

With this end in view, Mr Despard and Mr Schmid, in the *Allen Gardiner*, visited the Chilian settlement of Sandy Point, in March 1859. On their arrival, leave was obtained from the Chilian governor for Mr Schmid to reside there till an opportunity should present itself for carrying out the plan which he had made. He accordingly remained there, receiving much kindness from every one, till the Indians came on a trading visit. Mr Schmid's account of the result of his interview with them is as follows :—

" The chief and other Indians declaring themselves willing and glad to let me go with them, I promised the chief

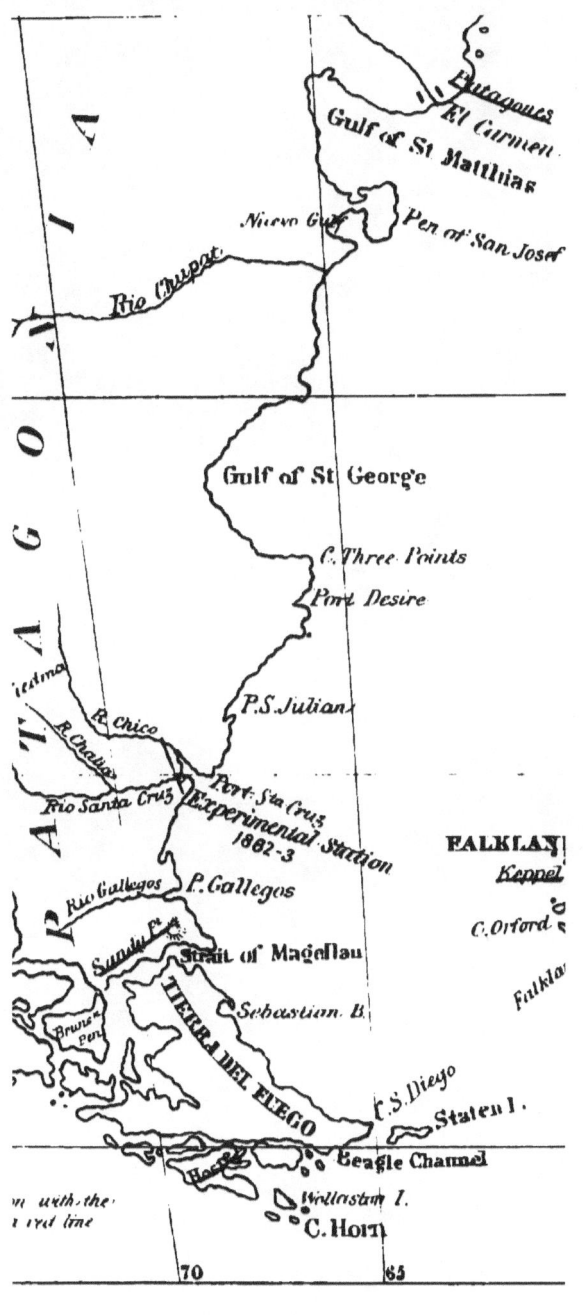

that if he would protect my person and property, supply me with sufficient food, and otherwise treat me well, I should pay him, on the return of the *Allen Gardiner*, one barrel of bread, one of flour, half a barrel of sugar, and tobacco; and that the vessel would bring presents to all the Indians. I wrote out the contract, read it to the Indians, and then delivered it to the governor, according to his request.

" It was Saturday, April 23, the sun shone brightly after two days' heavy rain, when I bade farewell to my friends, who had shown me so much kindness during my stay here, and then to the governor, who took much trouble to insure my safety and welfare during my wanderings with these Indians. This done, I left the colony, riding between my new companions, and talking to those who knew a little Spanish. Trusting in the omnipresence of Him whom the heavens cannot contain, I went on. Little, however, did I think I should have to travel such a distance that day, and several hours of the night. From the colony, our road was along the beach, at the edge of the wood, and a horrible road it was ; trunks of trees lay in the way, and it was necessary to go over large slippery stones. So we went on till we came towards Laredo Bay, then through swamps and water for many miles. When I was standing before the tent which was now my shelter, many Indians were sitting or standing round the fire, ready to look upon the unexpected stranger that had so suddenly come to them. When they had satisfied their curiosity they dispersed each to his tent. Weary, I laid myself down, but I rose refreshed, having slept well.

" The chief, Ascaik, with whom I live, has a son about twenty-four years old, called Gemoki; it is with him that I go when we move from place to place, but when we are in the encampment I live in Ascaik's tent. He calls me his son, and his children call me their brother.

" During the first three months our encampments were

in the neighbourhood of Gregory Range, because in winter
the guanacoes frequent that place, and we should most likely
have remained there all the winter, had it not been for the intelligence that was brought to Ascaik, that many ostriches
were seen about the east end of Gregory Range; so next
day we left to travel northward. We wandered several successive days, until we arrived off the entrance to the straits,
where the Indians found a wreck, a fine barque of iron,
called the *Anne Baker*, of Liverpool. It was already late
and dark when Gemoki and I came to our new encampment, which was about half a mile from where the wreck was.
Most of the Indians had arrived, had gone to the wreck,
found wine, and were terribly intoxicated. It was a terrible
night; few of the Indians went to bed. It was said that
two men were killed, and others wounded, in drunken brawls.

Travelling northward again, we met two chiefs, Kaili and
Watchi, with some other Indians coming from the neighbourhood of Rio Negro. Casimiro* arrived a few days after. The
Indians prepared themselves to give him a distinguished reception. They saddled their best and finest horses, and
arrayed themselves in their gayest dresses, and those who had
lances set them up; others armed themselves with muskets
or fowling-pieces, which they fired when they met Casimiro.
As soon as Casimiro saw me he called me, and invited me to
his house, where he entertained me with guanaco meat, which
he cooked and prepared with his own hands. He showed
me two papers which the captains of two men-of-war had
given him, one in English by Captain Rowan, and the other
in French by Captain Gros. Both speak well of him, and
recommend him to other captains for his dealing honestly
in the sale of guanaco flesh. Owing to his knowledge of
Spanish, and his visits to Chili, he is a man of some influence with these Patagonians, but he is not considered a chief,

* This man had said that he would welcome a teacher for his people.

although he is inclined to give himself out as one. Kaili and Watchi are chiefs, acknowledged as such, like Ascaik, and related to him. These men told us that many of their children had died on the way, which news made the encampment a scene of lamentations among the women.

" Next day we were again on the move towards the wreck, where, after six days walking, we arrived. Then scenes of drunkenness were again renewed till we left the place.

" You will, no doubt, be anxious to know what progress I have made in the acquisition of the Patagonian language. I have progressed so far that I can ask many little things and speak a little, but to converse is not in my power yet. I am obliged to learn by listening to others, for those who speak Spanish know it so imperfectly that they do not understand what I ask. There is one man who is very ready to tell me the Indian for Spanish if he knows it, and understands the latter, but I cannot persuade him to teach me every day. If I wish to know the name of a thing or action, I ask those who do not know Spanish at all by saying, *Kete amu win?* what do you call this?

" In regard to religion, their minds and understandings are dark. God, the living God, and Maker of all things, is not known to them. Nor do they worship any other object, or acknowledge a Supreme Being. Their lamentations over the dead are generally very affecting, and their demonstrations of grief so loud that they can be heard at a distance."

Mr Schmid gives the following anecdote of Ascaik :—

" On one occasion some seamen belonging to the Chilian colony were returning home from a wreck. They were without food for some time, and their way to the colony was yet a long one. Ascaik, as soon as he heard of their being in the neighbourhood, brought the case before me. He proposed that two or three should go with him, each with a spare horse, on which to bring the sailors over. Accordingly,

Ascaik, Kaili, and two other men went, and in the meantime some of the women made up the fires, and set about
preparing a pot of rice, with which to regale their expected
hungry guests. The fact of my having lived among them for
so many months, and this anecdote of Ascaik, are very encouraging."

Mr Schmid arrived at Sandy Point in February 1859.
When the year came round, and the schooner had not arrived
with the necessary supplies for himself, and the promised presents for the Indians, he felt his position to be no longer tenable,
especially as the noble-minded chief Ascaik had died suddenly.
Mr Schmid did not know how sad and sufficient a cause
withheld the vessel from coming as expected, and as he had
no means of going to the Falklands to inquire, and to confer
with Mr Despard, he gladly accepted the offer of a passage to
Valparaiso. Here he received much kindness and hospitality
from Mr Dennett, the chaplain, and went thence to England.

The following year he went out again, joined his fellow-
labourer, Mr Hunziker, at Keppel Island, and with him
arrived at Sandy Point on the 10th of June 1861. They
were kindly welcomed by the governor, and by Mr Schmid's
former friends in the colony. On the 27th of July they left
Sandy Point, in company with Casimiro and a few other
Patagonians, and arrived at the encampment of the main
body on the banks of the river Gallegos on the 18th of
August. The chiefs were much pleased with the presents
brought them, and behaved in a very friendly manner,
Gemoki in particular never omitting to give them some
ostrich meat when he came in from hunting. Casimiro in-
trusted his two sons to the missionaries for instruction, and
Galbez, the eldest, behaved very well, but the other appeared
to be slow and indolent. On September 14 Mr Schmid writes:
—" I am given to understand that the Indians feel great
sympathy with Casimiro's younger boy, because they think

that his father sold him to us, and that he is now our slave.
Now, let me describe the slavery to which these two boys are
subjected. They sleep on a better bed, and in a warmer
tent than they were used to. They live with us, and share
everything we have. We supply them with decent clothes;
they receive instruction in reading, writing, and speaking
English; they fetch two or three kettles of water. These Indians are an ignorant, and yet withal a mischievous set."

The missionaries continued to move from place to place
with the Indians till the 9th of November, when, stiff and
weary from a long day's ride, they again arrived at the
Chilian colony. On the 12th, Mr Schmid distributed the
rest of the things which, by agreement, were to be given to
the natives for their former kind treatment of him; and he
writes on the 13th :—

"This evening came Gemoki's mother, and brought no less
than five bags, expecting that I would fill them with provisions. In consideration of past kindness I gave her some
biscuit and some rice, but not enough to fill even two bags—
far from it. The more one gives this people the more they
ask.

"Let me now tell you our daily routine. On getting up,
we had morning worship; and, that the Indians might see
what we were doing, we opened the tent: this was not necessary, because they came often before we were ready, creeping
in underneath. Whilst we were at prayer, we were often
watched by men, women, and children; some were silent,
others talked or made some noise, some wanted to talk
with us, to borrow some tool, or call our attention to something else. We told them repeatedly not to disturb us, but
scarcely a day passed without some unpleasantness of this
kind whilst we read a portion of God's Word, and offered up
prayers. Casimiro's two boys, who were with us, joined us
in our worship, and knelt. We neither have, nor can have,

a fixed hour for meals as long as we live this disagreeably unsteady life. We dressed the boys in shirt, trousers, and a blouse. We taught them to be clean and orderly, and so far they made satisfactory progress. When we were not engaged in teaching the boys, I collected words, arranged them, and tried if I could not discover some grammatical construction. I am now in possession of 1050 words."\

After so much experience of Indian life, the missionaries took passage to the Falkland Islands for Christian intercourse and advice. Having now made some progress in the language, it was thought better to have a fixed place of residence in one of those places which the Patagonians are in the habit of frequenting on their hunting excursions, in the hope that some others might be induced to follow the example of Casimiro, and entrust their sons to the missionaries for instruction.

Captain Gardiner and Mr Schmid had, at different times, with the same object, entered Patagonia from the extreme south. Both found reason to doubt the expediency of working from thence. The net was to be cast on the other side. The north seemed to present wider and more reliable opportunities of access to the Indians. But before moving the basis of operations entirely from the Straits of Magelhaen to the Rio Negro, a preliminary attempt was made to form a station at Santa Cruz.

The river Santa Cruz is in latitude 50° S., and flows from the Andes to the Atlantic, a distance of about 200 miles. The valley of the river, flanked by step-formed terraces, is supposed to have been formerly a strait of the sea, like that of Magelhaen, joining the Atlantic and Pacific Oceans. The current of the river is strong. In 1834, when the late Admiral, then Captain, Fitz-Roy, explored the river, it took seventeen days of hard towing to ascend 140 miles, while four days sufficed to bring the explorers back to the point of departure. The country is barren, and, except in the valleys, where streams of fresh water are found, wears an arid and bronzed complexion. Guanacoes and ostriches are frequently seen in large numbers, yet on the whole the Indians consider game scarce in that district, and do not consequently resort much to it. Pasturage, too, for their horses is not abundant. The puma is very common, and a small fox; geese, swans, and ducks of many kinds, swarm on some of the lakes, a few leagues from the coast.

The climate is undoubtedly healthy. The prevailing winds are, more or less, westerly. The rain-fall is slight. On the western coast of Patagonia, on the slopes of the Cordilleras, the rain-fall is very great, and there is in consequence a plentiful vegetation. Throughout the vast territory of Patagonia, however, eastward of the Cordilleras, the case is very different. Here, if we except the valleys of a few rivers, the appearance of the country is hopelessly barren. The rain-bearing clouds formed in the Antarctic circle are attracted by the mountains of Tierra del Fuego, and Western Patagonia, and on them empty out all the moisture with which they are so heavily charged ; hence the wooded aspects of these high lands. The intumescence of the atmosphere, consequent upon the discharge of moisture from the air, is constant and great, and causes, probably, those heavy gales which make Cape Horn so formidable. But, dried in their passage over the mountains referred to, the prevailing south-west winds descend upon the plains of Patagonia with no fertilising power, only to revel over their parched surface, and create the blinding dust-storms so common in that land.

The attempt to form a mission station in the neighbourhood of the Santa Cruz river was experimental. It had already been proved, by the experience of Messrs Schmid and Hunziker, that no permanently good effect could be looked for from the necessarily irregular efforts to instruct the Indians, made during their wild life in the plains. A place, and a plan, where and by which an orderly course of instruction could be carried on, seemed to be primary conditions of success. Accordingly, in May 1862, the rudiments of a station were formed at Weddell's Bluff. The hope was cherished that Indians might be attracted to the spot, and the nucleus formed of a future settlement.

On June 1, 1862, Mr Schmid thus reports his arrival in those parts:—"After a stormy passage of ten days from Keppel Island, we anchored in Santa Cruz river-mouth. The point of the southern bank presented no favourable locality for a station, there being neither water nor grass, and it having other disadvantageous characteristics. We moved, therefore, ten miles up the estuary, and anchored off Weddell's Bluff. Here, on examination, we found a fine sheltered valley, with a running stream of good water, good and abundant grass, and plenty of fuel. . . . . To-morrow we shall begin to erect our cottage."

On August 11 Mr Schmid speaks of the first visit received from the Indians :—" I have the pleasure of informing you that the Indians are in the neighbourhood. They have supplied two vessels which happened to be lying in the river with guanaco meat. One of the captains came up here yesterday with an Indian, about 8.30 P.M. They remained over night, and returned this morning to the vessel. The Indian was a stranger to me, having never been south of Santa Cruz before. He asked me my name, and when I told him he remembered it, having heard it from others who came from the south two years ago. There is an encampment of them on the north shore, and there are some among them who know me, having been down south when I was first amongst them. . . . . I do not think we have anything to fear from these Indians. They speak the language, a great part of which I have learned."

The visits of vessels to Santa Cruz are few and far between, but an opportunity of sending a letter occurred some two months after the above was written, and from it we gather that Mr Schmid had determined to travel with his new Indian acquaintances to the southward, in order to induce, if possible, some of his southern friends to visit Santa Cruz, and place their children under the instruction of himself and Mr Hunziker.

The journey of Mr Schmid was long and wearisome, lasting sixteen days. The effect of the solitude on Mr Hunziker in his absence was painful. They had, however, been content to submit to loneliness and wanderings in order to prepare the way for the entrance of the gospel of Christ amongst the heathen. Not till the first week in December did Mr Schmid return to Weddell's Bluff, accompanied by Casimiro, and having a promise from the tribe whom he had been visiting that in some two months they would reach the mission station.

On New-Year's Day 1863 the *Allen Gardiner*, on her voyage from England to the Falklands, entered the Santa Cruz river to visit the missionaries. " That day was to us a day of joy," writes Mr Schmid. Eleven months had elapsed since any letter from their friends, or relations, or from the committee, had reached them. The isolation of their position, the delay in the approach of the mission schooner, which had been looked for since October, and the disappointment consequent on the non-arrival of the Indians, had proved very trying to the faith and patience of the brethren at Santa Cruz.

Our readers can scarcely have failed to observe the peculiar difficulties of missionary work in Patagonia. The natives have no fixed abodes, and move over the vast ranges of the wilderness according to the requirements of the chase, or of pasture, or it may be of trade. For in the extreme north of Patagonia, on the Rio Negro, and in the extreme south, at

Sandy Point, these Indians seek an opportunity for disposing of the spoils of the chase, bartering their splendid ostrich robes and feathers, and guanaco mantles, &c., for spirits, and rice, and sugar, and cutlery, and tobacco. In order to draw them with any certainty to a particular locality, it seems necessary to afford this nomad race an opening for barter. No arrangement of this kind was made in connexion with the experimental mission station on the Santa Cruz; and the difficulty of making it a centre of attraction for the Indians was in proportion to their inability to comprehend the prospective advantages of the instruction offered. On the arrival of the *Allen Gardiner* with the superintendent missionary on board, this matter necessarily received his attention, and by him was submitted to the committee in England for their serious consideration. It was suggested that, without trespassing upon the duties assigned to the missionaries, collateral arrangements might be made for a regulated system of barter, whereby, with great advantage to the Indians, and the certainty of drawing them into the neighbourhood of the station, the hands of the missionaries might be strengthened, and the objects for which they had come be greatly furthered. Such a plan was not of course free from theoretical objections, and would have demanded great caution in its execution, but it was, perhaps, worth a trial, being almost essential to success under the circumstances of the projected work on the Santa Cruz. With these preliminary remarks, we give portions of Mr Stirling's journal on the occasion of his visit in January 1863 :—

" The estuary of the Santa Cruz was entered on the evening of January 1, 1863, and on the following morning I landed at Weddell's Bluff, and received a most cordial welcome from our fellow-workers there located. It removed a weight of anxiety to find them well, for it had not been without many anxious thoughts that my mind contemplated the

possible inconvenience imposed on them by the tardy approach of the *Allen Gardiner*, yet we had lost no time that it
was in our power to save. . . . . If energetically supported, the mission at Santa Cruz is, in my opinion, likely to
lead to important results. The work of your missionaries is ♪
a life-labour; there is no hurrying it on. The sphere of
action is too quiet to gratify those who yearn after stirring
dramatic movement, but it has all the richness and fulness of
the life of faith, and has a heroism of its own. The site of
the station is good, within a few yards of high-water mark,
and at the mouth of a valley which retreats towards the south-
west for a considerable distance inland. A stream of pure
water flows perennially through the valley, and a broad belt
of grass, offering fine pasture for cattle, gives a cheerful and
fertile aspect to the low land. The hills on either side are
intersected with ravines, or lift up their bronzed faces out of
some intervening dale, and refresh the air with the aroma of
shrubs and plants growing everywhere about them. . . . .
Messrs Schmid and Hunziker occupy what was formerly Mr
Gardiner's hut on Keppel Island. It is very small, but two
compartments have been added, one for sleeping, the other
for cooking purposes. The tent was pitched, and used as a
kind of store for such goods as would not excite cupidity in
the Indians, or suffer from comparative exposure. The white
canvas of the tent, and the English ensign waving its welcome
from the flag-staff; a neatly-thatched goat-house, whose
sleek tenants were picturesquely browsing on the hill-side by
the water; and a fine stock of firewood, industriously provided for the coming winter, gave an air of cheerfulness and
comfort to the scene of the first Protestant Christian mission
in Patagonia. The meeting with these brethren in Christ
was a most happy one to us all."

During the stay of the *Allen Gardiner* in the river, no
Indians made their appearance, much to the disappointment

of everybody. Nevertheless, it had been a period of refreshment to all. On January the 28th the vessel sailed for Keppel Island. "On the Sunday before our departure," writes the superintendent, "we celebrated the Lord's Supper in the cabin of the *Allen Gardiner*, having many times before joined together in prayer for the Divine guidance and blessing." It was not till the middle of May that the *Allen Gardiner* was again off Weddell's Bluff, and still the Indians were away hunting. In consequence, the disappointment and depression of spirit on the part of the missionaries there located were very great. On the following morning, however, the long-expected Indians made their appearance, an account of which, and the subsequent interviews with them, are found in the subjoined portions of the journals of the superintendent. It will be seen that Mr Stirling deemed it expedient to provide refreshment and change for the missionaries, and that they were accompanied to Keppel Island by three members of the southern tribe of Patagonians :—

"On Tuesday morning the captain announced from the deck the signal fires of the Indians, distant some three miles along the beach. There were two men, two lads, a woman, and an interesting little girl four years old. They promised the arrival in a few days of a numerous body of Indians, some 800 of whom were encamped not many miles off. The new-comers were soon entertained at the little station with coffee and biscuit, and the most friendly sentiments were exchanged. Like all Indians who are brought in contact with Europeans in these parts, one of them asked for brandy, and I scarcely think he believed me when we assured him that we had none; but some lime juice he greatly relished. His son came on board with him, a nice, well-conducted, good-looking lad. To my surprise, he expressed a wish to visit the Falklands, to see the governor, and so on; this wish he again and again expressed, as also that his daughter and son should accompany him. Mr Schmid carefully explained to him that the governor of the Falklands gave no brandy to the Indians, and that our mission station was very far away from where the governor lived; with these explanations he was quite content, but still wished to go in the ship. This posture of affairs suggested to my mind a release from the difficulties affecting the conduct of the mission in Patagonia.

" On Wednesday morning some Indians appeared on the heights overlooking the station, and then in picturesque groups descended to the position which we occupied. On Thursday the number of arrivals rapidly increased, so that some four hundred must have been present by night-fall. The leading chief of the southern Indians is Gemoki, son of Ascaik, the faithful ally of Mr Schmid during his first sojourn amongst the Patagonian Indians. I slept on shore that night, in order to form some estimate of the probable conduct of the Indians now bivouacked around the Crimean hut of our missionary brethren. Once I went out and took a view of the scene in the moonlight. The camp fires, still burning at uncertain intervals, and the baying of the dogs, alive to every strange footfall, contrasted strangely with the gloom of night, and the slumbering forms of many men crouched around the gray embers of the burnt-out wood. A hard frost had set in, and no unfrequent coughing showed that the effects of exposure were not to be disguised even amongst this hardy people. They had in fact come in most instances without their tents, a report of the presence of the *Allen Gardiner* at Santa Cruz having reached them somewhat unexpectedly, and drawn them to our station in irregular groups, according to the time and place at which they received the news, and the temper of the individuals interested in the matter. The neighbourhood of Weddell's Bluff was occupied by the advance guard of the Indians, whose main camp was pitched some fifteen miles to the south-west. Mr Schmid acted for me as interpreter, and most efficiently: through him I communicated to the chiefs and influential persons of the tribe the great objects of our coming to them, and in particular our desire to form a school for their children, and to have some of their families resident, or at any rate frequent visitors, at the station. Our wishes were to be made known throughout the camp, and on Friday morning a reply was to be given. The time arrived and I took my seat outside the house, Mr Schmid being on my right hand, Gemoki on my left. Casimiro was placed immediately before me, and all about him in a semicircle were seated on the ground some fifty men. Here and there were groups of Indians engaged in conversation, or watching us from a distance.

"After presents had been given and received, the question of forming a school for the Indian children was formally opened, and many pros and cons were stated. It was my endeavour to dispel from the minds of this people any suspicions of sinister dealing on our part, and to persuade them of the simplicity of our object in coming to teach them about the 'true God, and Jesus Christ, whom He had sent;' not to occupy their territory; not to display the power of foreigners; not even to trade, was our great purpose; but to instruct them about another life, and a better world which lies beyond the grave. We wished to see the Indians numerous and happy, becoming, as Mr Schmid translated my meaning, a great nation. We were Christians, English Christians, not Spanish, not Chilian ; and our single object was their good. In reply, Casimiro, who acted as spokesman, said, ' the neighbourhood was not good for hunting ; that it was the intention of the people to go northward in the winter ; that for himself he should like his own children to be instructed, but that others would not promise. When would the ship be back again ?'

We answered, in about two months, wind and weather permitting. They then said they intended to remain in the district about that time, and expressed frequently and anxiously their desire that the *Allen Gardiner* would be again at Santa Cruz before their departure.

" You thus see a summary of our first formal palaver ; other palavers took place, but in the main the results were the same. The Indians would make no promises, especially Casimiro, who in fact was rather jealous, Mr Schmid told me, of instruction being offered to any but his own children. He wished to augment a waning influence at our expense. The issue did not disappoint me. I should have been less satisfied if the Indians had made full and free promises of agreeing to our proposals. They do not understand now the nature of those benefits which we seek to confer upon them : and they have had too much experience of the duplicity of so-called Christians to place themselves unhesitatingly under their control. It is not therefore surprising that they should be cautious in accepting our novel and disinterested proposals, the aim and scope of which glimmer doubtfully on the horizon of their minds. My own view of the matter is, however, far from gloomy. I see a people presenting many most interesting features of character, a fine race, barbarous indeed, and superstitious, but practising no cruel rites, and shut out of the pale of the Church of Christ, not from hostility to its truths, but by the perverse example of a conquering race too little amenable to the precepts of the gospel. The language of the people is now familiar to our missionaries, who have gained their confidence by the blameless character of their lives while wandering with them for months together, away from all European presence, over the hunting grounds of the south. I see, too, the children of this people capable of instruction, giving every indication of intelligence, and offering a most inviting field for sowing the seed of the

Word of God. No heart that ever loved a child could fail to acknowledge the appeal which the little bright-faced Patagonian children make for a share in one's interest and natural affection ; and to us, as Christians, what does not this appeal mean ? . . . . Our friends, Mr Schmid and Mr Hunziker, were quite at home with this people. Evidently in possession of their good will, and recognised as honorary members of the southern tribe, ' Ophilo,' (Mr Schmid) and ' Fred-rik,' (Mr Hunziker) were introduced to a northern chief as attached to the Tsonica of the south. We reached Keppel Island on May 29. The three natives were rather sick, but behaved very well."

Two persons were left in charge of the mission property at Santa Cruz in the absence of the missionaries ; and the hope was entertained that, the Indians having now been attracted to the spot, and put in possession of their wishes and intentions, the work might be resumed, and expanded in accordance with the experience gained.

Respecting the sojourn of the three Patagonians on Keppel Island Mr Schmid thus writes :—" My last letter informed you of our arrival at Keppel Island, whither we had gone from Santa Cruz for a little refreshment, by intercourse with our friends residing there. Platero, who is an old friend of mine, had asked to come with his daughter Mariquita and his son Belokon. The Fuegians, already there, were not a little surprised to see Patagonians come to Keppel. No intercourse took place between them, for they could not understand each other except by signs, and our Patagonians rather looked down upon their Fuegian neighbours. Platero, the father, was anxious that his son should learn to read and write, and be instructed generally ; and when the lad was receiving his lessons would often stand beside him and encourage him kindly to apply himself to the task before him. I explained to them the origin of our Sabbath ; why we set

apart one day in seven for the especial worship of God, and
do no work on that day. They attended divine service regularly every Sunday during their stay at Keppel."

With regard to the Patagonian language, Mr Schmid
writes:—" I have prepared a vocabulary, arranging the
words in alphabetical order, and an outline of grammar; a
considerable enlargement of that which was printed in 1860.
It is all written in the usual alphabet; for, as the inventors
of the phonetic system are always changing their alphabet,
I thought it best to do without it, and I should therefore
not like to return to phonetic. The words which I have
collected have been subjected to several tests, and they have
come out true and genuine; but as for abstract words, I
am getting more and more convinced that there is nothing
which could enable us to set before the Indians the truths of
our holy religion."

On the 1st of July the *Allen Gardiner*, with the superintendent on board, left Keppel Island for the Rio Negro, in the
north of Patagonia. Ten days after, Mariquita was taken ill,
and died suddenly. This caused deep regret to every one at
the station. "When the old father," says Mr Schmid, " saw
that his daughter had actually ceased to exist, he gave vent
to his grief in wailing, and singing doleful strains, as their
manner is. Belokon also cried bitterly for his sister, for they
were greatly attached to each other. The bereaved father
laid the blame on some Indian whose name he mentioned to
me, saying that he had killed her by witchcraft. This idea
is deeply rooted in their minds. Many Indians regard each
other with suspicion, and are very much afraid of being
killed by witchcraft. It is not mere talking that will convince them of the error and folly of their belief. Mariquita
died on Saturday evening, and was buried on Monday at
noon. That morning and the day following Platero went up
and down among the hills singing a dirge. I went and

fetched him, and tried to soothe his grief by assuring him of our deepest sympathies with him in his affliction. In the evening we had a prayer-meeting, at which we supplicated our heavenly Father that He would in His own wise providence overrule this sad event to the furtherance of the cause, and to the glory of His name. . . . . Platero was present listening, or rather watching our proceedings. He assured us of his friendship. Mariquita was not ill, he said, but bewitched by the Indians, and killed by them. They had killed his wife, and would kill him too."

But it is time to direct the reader's attention to another point of interest in connexion with the work of the mission. This is Patagones, or El Carmen, on the Rio Negro, in the north of Patagonia. In December 1862, on her voyage out from England to the Falklands, the *Allen Gardiner* visited this river, and two young men were located there with the view of acquiring first the Spanish, and next the Indian language. In Tierra del Fuego, and in the south of Patagonia, the Protestant missionary has little to fear from Roman Catholic influence. But in the north he comes into contact not only with an Indian, but a Spanish-speaking and Roman Catholic population. Accordingly, some of the early difficulties at Patagones arose from the opposition of the padre, and the suspicions of the Indians aroused by this man's jealousy, and active interference.

Some few years short of a century ago, certain colonists from old Spain formed a settlement on the Rio Negro; but it is now included in the Argentine Confederation, and, if we except the projected Welsh colony on the River Chupat, some 200 miles farther south, is its last outlying post of civilisation in that direction. The settlement is intersected by the river Negro. The name Patagones includes both divisions of the settlement ; that on the north side is called *El Carmen ;* that on the south, *El Merced.* The inhabitants are much knit together by family ties ; but here, as in other parts of the Confederacy, an immigrant class is being introduced, and the genius of the place begins to be disturbed.

During five months of the year Indians from all parts come in to trade. Here they bring for sale their manufactured woollen goods, ponchos, and cloths, and robes of various kinds, patterns, and colours. Here, too, they supply themselves with spirits, and yerba, and sugar, and other things. They, as a matter of course, are relentlessly cheated and spoiled. A resident in a neighbouring town to the north-east, who had been seriously injured by a foray of the Indians, in which they had swept off some 10,000 sheep, opened a store in the town in order to compensate himself by " trading" with them. The feeling towards the Indians, on the part of the Spanish-speaking population, is generally one of mingled hatred, fear, and contempt. That missionaries should come from England to instruct them seemed at first hardly conceivable, and many sagacious explanations were ventured on which could scarcely be brought into accord with the integrity of the missionaries' profession.

A few leagues from Patagones is an Indian *tolderia*, or village of tents. The inhabitants are rather more than 200. The men are in the pay of the government, being what are termed " mansos," or tame, and watch the frontier along with the regular troops against the independent tribes. Several of these " Indios mansos" have been baptized, but no instruction in the Christian faith has been seriously given, and they mingle a few popish ceremonies with their own superstitious rites at their religious festivals.

All these Indians are famous for their horsemanship, and present a strong contrast to the canoe Indians of Tierra del Fuego ; but there are affinities of race, and persons acquainted with the former have, when introduced to the

Fuegian lads who visited England in 1865, supposed that
they belonged to them. In stature the fisher Indians of the
south are dwarfish ; in Chili the Indian race is below our
average stature. In the north of Patagonia the aborigines
are not tall ; yet in the south of that country, next neighbour to the Fuegian, inserted and wedged in between men
physically smaller than himself, is the so-called Patagonian
giant. The representative of a *mere fragment* of people, he
there stands out with a grand average height of five feet ten
—a physical anomaly—a fault in the physiological strata of
South American races.

In ascending from the southern Archipelago through the
plains of Patagonia to the Pampas beyond, there are religious
as well as physical contrasts to be observed. The Fuegian
has no name for God, and no worship ; all is blank in this
respect. The Patagonian proper betrays in his funereal rites
a belief in a future state, and presents in his traditions,
although too languidly for practical expression, traces of the
old sun-worship. Higher up, the Indian of the Pampas holds
strongly his faith in the good and evil spirit, and seeks to
propitiate both by gifts and sacrifices. In his journeyings
over the lonely plains, as often as he sights the Ombu tree
he greets it with shoutings, and, ere he passes, leaves upon
the altar of the Unseen—for so he regards it—some tribute
of respect. Is he well to do ? he sacrifices a horse, or pours
spirits as a libation about the roots. Is he poor ? a cigar,
it may be, or a thread drawn from his poncho, indicates his
reverential awe. Once a year, however, a great religious
festival takes place—a festival which is probably the only
bond that now preserves these thinned and scattered tribes
from losing even the semblance of national life. It occurs
about midsummer, and is preceded by preliminary cere-
monials of three days' duration. A solemn parliament is
held, and questions affecting the Indian commonwealth are

discussed—questions of peace and war, of supply and demand, of health and sickness, of the favour and disfavour of the Supreme Being, of sacrifice to Him, and sacrifice to the devil, (Wallechu.) These things being settled, dancing follows— dancing for three days; no intoxicating drinks are allowed at this period. The excitement which follows arises from religious fervour. The lances of the Indians are planted in the ground, forming a long file of glittering steel, midway in which are two lances, distinguished the one by its white, the other by its black flag floating in the air. If you see three flags, the third being red, the Parliament has decided on war, and the Deity is invoked to give a blessing on the projected enterprise. Two young girls stand constantly in front of the banner-bearing lances, having in their hands vessels containing spirits, which ever and anon they sprinkle reverently towards the symbolic standards. Headed by two women playing tambourines, the whole company of Indian females dance round the file of lances; the men, again, in an outer column, move likewise in the dance, but in a direction the reverse of the women. Thus, if the females pass from right to left, the men move from left to right, so that in two orbits, and separately directed, the dance revolves about the lance-line as an axis. The voice of the entire multitude is meanwhile lifted up in prayer and singing, and the air rings strangely with outbursts of religious fervour, and a rude chorus of superstitious sentiment. These things having lasted three days, the sacrifice is appointed for the next dawn, when a prayer is offered by the priest for special blessings.

They offer in sacrifice two young animals, always males, either two colts or foals, two calves, or two lambs. The living animal is cut open, and the heart is taken out and held up to the sun by the appointed priest, words being uttered significant of the hearts of the people being God's, and offered to Him accordingly. The sacrifice takes place always at daybreak.

During the three days when dancing prevails, and the women stop to rest, the men mount their horses, and ride round in a large circle, beating all kinds of noisy instruments, to frighten away the evil spirit. This mounted corps is preceded by two horses, one white, the other black, (the black horse having a ring of white paint round his eyes, and the white having a ring of black,) and both being covered with such things as when shaken produce a jargon of sounds. In this rude fashion do these Indian tribes express their dependence on the Most High, and worship the Invisible as He is represented by the sun and moon. The white and black flags, and the white and black horses, have doubtless a symbolic meaning; and the dance, too, represents probably the apparent motions of the heavenly bodies, and the great circles in which they move.

The Indians south of the Rio Negro are called Tchuelche, and their language it is of which Mr Schmid has made a dictionary and grammar, and to print which in the Spanish form the government of Buenos Ayres expressed a desire This government, we may here state, is not only tolerant, but liberal in opinion; and in 1863, when appealed to in connexion with the mission work on the Rio Negro, promised, through the Minister of the Interior, "all the moral support in its power" to the then superintendent of the mission.

The Pampas Indians to the north of Patagonia are principally under two chiefs—one Cafalcura, the other Rowke. The former has 600 spears at his immediate command, and can on great occasions rally 2000 to his standard. The Indians on the banks of the Negro chiefly occupy districts near the Cordilleras. They are called " Chilenos " by the people of Patagones, and speak the Chilidugu language, and are said to be more numerous than the other tribes east of the

Andes. *Las Mansanas*—so called from the apple-trees there abounding near the sources of the Rio Negro—appear to be their head-quarters. The government is pursuing a conciliatory policy with respect to these various tribes, seeking by treaties and bounties to keep them from disturbing the country. The purpose of the government is to encourage immigration to the utmost, and tranquillity is essential to secure this. It is natural, therefore, that the pacificatory work of a Christian mission should be regarded with favour by the rulers of the country. As the civilised population increases, the aboriginal will be pressed more and more back towards the Cordilleras, and towards the south; and the government will probably offer inducements to the Indians, as their territory contracts about them, to adopt fixed stations, and pastoral pursuits. It was then for the benefit of these interesting races that a basis of missionary work was formed at Patagones. The first efforts of the missionaries were to master the Spanish language; and this done, to attempt to get hold of the Indian dialects. Again, we must impress upon our readers the necessity of patience.

We spoke in an early part of this chapter of the opposition of the padre. The poor man is no longer living. In his last illness, he was attended by the Rev. George Humble, M.D., a medical missionary, who, in October 1864, undertook the work at Patagones. But we are glad to record that for many months before the padre's decease there was a softening down of his hostility to the Protestant missionaries. In the first instance, he denounced the circulation of the Scriptures in Spanish, and visited houses even some leagues from the town, forbidding the people to read the Bible, or to receive the distributors of it. Either because this course did not answer, or because his own mind underwent a change, he ceased his opposition, and granted permission to his flock to read the once forbidden book. His early attempts to set the Indians against the missionaries did not, in the long run, succeed, although, for a while, they retarded the work; for the local authorities were required, in consequence, by the central government, to re-assure the Indians of the friendly purposes of the missionaries.

Encouraged by these circumstances, a plan was formed for a mission-house, and school, and dormitory, and an appeal for funds was made to friends in Buenos Ayres. Upwards of £100 were at once provided for this special purpose in that quarter; and with a grant from home the work was proceeded with. In those out-of-the-world parts everything moves slowly. The ox-cart, with its huge wheels, is there the most progressive thing. If, however, *adobes* and roof-beams, and window-frames, take long in coming into shape, and the school is but a thing of the future, the Indians could nevertheless be visited in their own dwellings, and if not instructed much at least be impressed with the objects of their would-be teachers. And so we find one of the missionaries writing:—" Mr Andres and I visited the tolderia, and read and explained passages of God's Word to the Indians. The parable of the Prodigal Son seemed to arrest much attention, and the Beatitudes were likewise listened to eagerly. When, borrowing our illustrations from things about us, we spoke of the sword of God being love, and the house of God being love, and the lance of God being love, and that Christ came not to destroy men's lives, but to save them, the glimmer of a new light seemed to pass over the minds of the listening group, and an expression of satisfaction found its way from more than one mouth." The presence of the missionaries excited curiosity and surprise everywhere, but there were not wanting signs that among some a thoughtful and earnest spirit lent its sanction and sympathy to their work. " I have had," writes Mr Stirling, " deeply interesting and pro-longed conversations with an Indian who belongs to Osorno in Araucania, but who is connected with, and much in the confidence of, the Indians of the Andes. He is a man of small stature, but keen and intelligent, a man of prudent counsels, and in favour of peace, if it can be honourably secured. The threatening of war arose out of a massacre of certain Indians in 1862 by the people of El Carmen. This man is most earnest in his entreaties for the location of a missionary among his own people. He would ' receive us with open arms.' ' Many sleepless nights,' he said, ' he spent thinking of the woes of his country.' As we talked together far into the night on the subject of our work and its special features, he expressed a desire that the conversation might continue all night, for we ' might not meet again,' and he longed to see his wishes fulfilled. Having slept on board the *Allen Gardiner*, (lying at anchor in the Rio Negro,) he was up before myself, ready to depart ; but asking permission to come into my berth, he most touchingly bade me good-bye, kissing my hand, and saying he regarded me henceforth as a brother."

Thus were the missionaries engaged in opening the way for the furtherance of the gospel in this portion of South America. But we must, while the preparations for a mission-house and school, &c., are still slowly progressing, withdraw the reader for a moment from the Rio Negro to the Santa Cruz River, in order that with renewed and concentrated attention he may return to the work at Patagones.

We have spoken of the station on the Santa Cruz as experimental. The time was at hand when the experiment could no longer be supported, and the missionaries retired from the scene. Messrs Schmid and Hunziker, as we have seen, had suffered from their stay in Patagonia, and sought rest and refreshment of body and mind at the Society's station on Keppel Island in the Falklands. They were now, however, ready to return to the scene of their labours, accom-

L

panied by the natives, who belonged to that part. The *Allen Gardiner* arrived at the Santa Cruz in due course, with the mission party on board. Great, however, was their sorrow on reaching the station to find that a vessel from Stanley, in the Falklands, had been in the river for some time, the captain of which, under a plea of trade, had debauched with rum and other spirits the Indians gathered in the neighbourhood by the influence of the missionaries ; and that, having set them in a state of restlessness and excitement, he had persuaded them to meet him in a few weeks at another spot for a similar process of trade. The ship, in consequence, was well freighted with ostrich robes and feathers, guanaco mantles, &c. The Indians were in no state of mind to profit by the counsels of their true friends, and their true friends were again filled with discouragement. Simultaneously letters from the committee reached the superintendent discountenancing his proposition and plan for giving an outlet, by a fair and regulated process of exchange, for the goods the Indians desired to part with; and as without some arrangement of this kind they could not be expected to visit the district regularly—in fact could not afford to do so—it became almost a necessity to abandon Santa Cruz as a basis of operation. This accordingly was done, and the *Allen Gardiner* having again reached the Rio Negro, bearing the missionary staff and property from Santa Cruz, the determination of the superintendent was to concentrate and direct the efforts of the Mission at and from Patagones.

Mr Schmid now visited England and Germany; was ordained deacon by the Bishop of London ; married, and then returned in company with the Rev. G. Humble, M.D., to renew the work. A position was assigned to him at Bahia Blanca, where an opening for usefulness presented itself; but, we regret to say, his health, never robust, having given way with dangerous symptoms, has compelled him recently to retire from that place. Mr Hunziker, having married, was stationed with Dr Humble at Patagones, and under their joint care the work has proceeded. The following extracts from the letters of Dr Humble indicate the progress of events. It will be seen that, bringing his medical abilities to bear, he has opened a dispensary in addition to the church, school, &c.

Under date of *June* 12, 1865, Dr Humble thus writes :— " The schools and church ought to have been opened by this time, but are not, owing to the slow progress of the work, and the difficulty of getting labourers. There is, however, but little more to be done to the building, and two or three weeks ought to see their completion. The mission-house, when finished, will be a solid, substantial, and by no means unsightly building; it will give this mission a permanent basis, and be a centre of operations from which branch missions may afterwards spring.

" My position as a medical man gives me opportunities of getting at the Indians which I should not otherwise possess. I trust I may have grace and wisdom given me so as to turn their minds from the earthly physician to the good Physician himself, who is able and willing to cure their souls with the healing balm of His own precious blood. I hope, too, that the friendly offices I am able to render to the Indians will give them confidence in our good intentions, and induce them to intrust some of their children to our care as soon as the schools are opened." The opening of the mission church is announced under date of August 17, 1865, and matters of faith are being thus gradually translated, as Mr Gardiner would say, into matters of fact. " The mission church on the south side of the river was opened last Sunday, August 13. Although the morning was wet and windy, the church was full ; had it been fine, I believe it would have been over-crowded. I read prayers and preached, Mr Hunziker read·

ing the lessons. We chanted the Venite, Jubilate, Gloria Patri, and the responses between the Commandments, and sang hymns appropriate to the occasion. Could the friends of our society at home have seen the church and congregation, it would have cheered their hearts, and they would have felt that a real work was going on in Patagones. . . . . I purpose opening the boy's school in a week or two, and am only waiting the completion of the building. I am not quite decided about a girl's school. I fear it will be impossible to get a Protestant teacher in this place. For some months past the measles have been raging here, both among adults and children. Being the only doctor in the place, you may fancy how important have been the demands made upon me. I have often hardly time to take my meals." More recently, Dr Humble thus gives a view of his congregation :—" A few Sundays ago we had the church almost full of Indians in their quaint costumes and painted faces—Tchuelche-Indians come for trade. I begin to find the Indian work very interesting; and as very many speak Spanish, I am able to converse with them, though not, of course, with proficiency."

In this way the work is being carried on, and we trust that our readers will not fail to supplicate the Divine blessing upon it. The work they have seen in its weaknesses and in its trials. But encouragements by the way have not been wanting. The labours of Captain Gardiner will not be in vain—nay, more, have not been in vain. Heaven, it has been said, is for those who fail on earth. Such failures as those of Gardiner and his companions do indeed point heavenwards. They are prophetic, too—the preludes of great triumphs; for the cross and the crown are in the counsels of Heaven intimately related. " Be thou faithful unto death, and I will give thee a crown of life."

Rº Tolten   L Villarien

ARAUCANIA

Rº Calle Calle   Valdivia

L. Rancô

Osorno

Places of Interest in connection with the
Mission are marked with a red line.

CHAPTER IX.

THE ESTABLISHMENT OF MISSIONARY CHAPLAINCIES IN
SOUTH AMERICA.

IT was in the year 1860, after the mission to Tierra del
Fuego had been put into working order, while Mr Despard
was residing at Keppel with several Fuegians under instruction, and the missionary schooner at his disposal, for further
visits to the coasts of Patagonia and Tierra del Fuego, that
an attempt was made to establish a mission among the
Indians of Chili, and Mr Allen W. Gardiner was appointed
by the committee as their first missionary to that country.
He had now been more than a year and a half in England,
had been admitted to holy orders by the Bishop of Gloucester and Bristol, had married, and had devoted several months
to the study of medicine.

He arrived at Valparaiso with his wife and child in July
1860, and intended, if possible, to settle at once in the Araucanian territory; but being assured by those who knew the
country that such a step was quite impracticable, he was
induced to take up a position at Lota as chaplain to a little
colony of our own countrymen, who were, for the most part,
engaged in working a coal mine. His object in availing
himself of this opening for ministerial work was not only the
sore need which existed for its exercise, but the hope that

ultimately it might lead to the formation of a missionary out-
post or station among the neighbouring Araucanian tribes,
when he should have won the confidence of Chilians and Indians, and dispelled the jealousy with which the latter regard
all foreigners, and which the former might be expected to feel
towards Protestant missionaries, seeing that the constitution
of Chili tolerated no religion but the Roman Catholic Apostolic, and even at Valparaiso the Protestants held their worship under sufferance.

The following is Mr Gardiner's description of Lota :—

"*October* 1860.—We are on a hill, prettily wooded down
to the sea-shore. From our front windows we see the dark
blue waters of the Pacific, and enjoy the magnificent sunsets.
The back of the house looks down upon a snug little valley,
with plenty of wood and water. Beyond is the hill of Villa
Grande, where Caupolican and his braves lie. He was, I believe, a native of Lota. The ruins of the old Spanish fort
are seen on the hill. The Indian road passes our house, but
the visits of the Indians are seldom made. It is a ride of
thirty miles to their grounds. This spot has been purchased
by a wealthy Chilian, who has built the largest mole which
exists in Chili. Ships of a thousand tons burden can load
alongside, and consequently this small, wild, picturesque place
is favoured with communications from England once a fort-
night, and from Valparaiso once a week."

The Gardiners had not time to settle themselves in their
new home before an alarm was given of an expected attack
from the distant Indians on the Indians of the neighbourhood. Arauco and Lota were thought to be in so much
danger that the authorities at Concepcion sent a ship to Valparaiso to report the critical state of affairs, and from thence
the telegraph conveyed a message to the Chilian government
at Santiago. In a very few days two steamers arrived at
Arauco Bay with troops, where they found the settlers and

friendly Indians making the best of their position in expectation of an attack, and so that danger was happily averted.

Two months after his arrival at Lota Mr Gardiner was able to report,—" The Sunday services held in our sitting-room are well attended, and about thirty children attend the Sunday-school." A beginning was thus made of church ministrations.

A school-room was built early in the following year through the kind assistance of English friends in Valparaiso. The day-school was opened on the first week in March 1861 with eight pupils, and the numbers gradually increased till every child of a suitable age attended. After this, a visit from Mr Balfour, (of the firm of Balfour & Williamson, of Liverpool,) who was then resident at Valparaiso, was very encouraging and refreshing to Mr Gardiner. He has elsewhere said,—" Without Mr Balfour's assistance the school could not have been built."

The school and the church services under his sole charge now occupied so much of his time that he wrote urgently to the committee for help, in order that the study of the languages might not be retarded by the pressure of daily work. This pressure was increased by the establishment of a dispensary. Mr Coombe arrived in October, and thus in few words described his first impressions :—" I found Mr Gardiner holding a sphere of usefulness far beyond anything I had expected." Intelligence of the work at Lota had also reached Santiago, where there are a considerable number of English, one of whom visited Mr Gardiner, and tried to persuade him to remove to Santiago, where he would find a welcome, a sphere of ministerial work, and a competence,

The following year, 1862, a further advance was made. Mr Coombe took charge of the boys' school. The services were well attended. A preliminary visit was made to the Indians. An infant school was established by Mrs Gardiner, with the aid of a pupil teacher, and a Christian work was commenced at Puchoco, another mining village in Arauco Bay, about five miles distant.

Mr Coombe thus wrote in 1863 :—"Our scholars continue regular in their attendance, always giving marked attention, and are making great progress. Two evenings of the week were employed in teaching the young men who are engaged in the mines by day, a third is devoted to a Bible-class, and a fourth to a prayer-meeting, which is always well attended, and much enjoyed by the people. It is pleasant to know that they all date their various changes of mind to the effects of Mr Gardiner's ministry among them. He has long wished an agency to be started for carrying the gospel to the sailors who visit this port; but the multiplicity of engagements which we have hitherto had in the erection of the station has prevented our doing anything in that branch of missionary work. Often there are as many as twelve and more ships in the port, and many of them commanded by English-speaking German captains, with a good percentage of English and German sailors among the crews. We have frequently had three captains of vessels at the Sunday service during the past winter."

In the year 1864 an infant school was established at Puchoco; Mr Keller arrived as a second catechist, to help forward the Indian work; and Mr Gardiner, a second time, declined to remove from Lota to Santiago. The terrible catastrophe which had occurred in one of the churches on the 8th of the previous December, causing the death of two thousand persons, through the accidental kindling of all the festival decorations for the Feast of the Conception, called attention to the melancholy ignorance of the gospel, which existed among the Spanish-speaking population. A pressure was put upon the committee of the South American Missionary Society to send a clergyman at once to Santiago, and a suggestion was made that Mr Gardiner would be acceptable there. He, however, felt that he could not entertain this suggestion, because it would remove him from that Indian work on which his heart was set, and for which he had already, as he thought, secured a basis: accordingly he declined the offer, and remained at his post. In the same year the Roman Catholic bishop of Concepcion commenced proceedings to stop the Lota work, especially the dissemination of Protestant books and Bibles, contending that it was a violation of the national laws. It is not necessary to enter here into the controversy, which was settled in 1865 by the erasure of that clause in the constitution which tolerated no religion but the Roman Catholic.

Mr Gardiner thus writes on the subject:—"As it is often darkest just before sunrise, owing to the collection of mists and vapours in the lower air, so my half-year of greatest difficulty and opposition was from January to June of this year, (1865.)'

"*July* 11.—Early in the morning a courier galloped into the courtyard of Sr. Saavedra's house, in which I was, with an express from Santiago, and it proved to be the news of religious toleration in Chili. As I returned home with the news, and saw the sun shining on the Pacific Ocean, I felt that the darkness had now passed, and that the true light might now shine in Chili. I remembered that on July the 11th, eleven years ago, I had stood by the banks of an English river to see an English schooner launched to carry the gospel-flag to South America, and such a victory, coming with the dawn of the same morning, seemed to speak of a light in the dark valley, a hope on the stormy sea, and a future race yet to be run and won by the South American Society. We are now the ministers of a district, and no longer only the masters of a village school."

Later in the same year he writes:—"The change in the Constitution of Chili, which enables us to read and write and speak freely on Protestant subjects, had hardly time to be perceptibly felt before the cause of civilisation, and with it the cause of evangelisation, has been temporarily embarrassed by the blockade of the Spaniards."

This embarrassment has now happily passed away; and the year, which began with a season of great sickness, and a controversial attack of unusual severity, called attention to the importance and efficiency of the Mission dispensary, and the great blessing which had attended the services and preaching in the Mission church, and the working of the Mission schools. But, while the church, school, and dispensary work at Lota made such gratifying progress, it was found that Lota was too distant from the Indian territory to form a suitable basis for a mission to the Araucanians. Mr Gardiner had again and again undertaken missionary journeys, and he had exchanged friendly visits with a powerful chief beyond the river Lebu, and this led to the formation of a station at Lebu for the more distant missionary work. But the enterprise required a scale of expenditure too great for the Society at that time to undertake. For the present, therefore, it has been abandoned, but not, we hope, for ever. There seems to be good reason for believing that the way is open for a mission to the interior, from Valdivia on the west, and from El Carmen on the east.

If we now turn to the ministerial side of the Lota station, we have before us the germ which, in 1864, developed into the larger proportions of a grand scheme for the supply of English chaplains to the various English settlers on both the east and the west coasts. The want was not supplied a day too soon. Thousands of our countrymen were scattered over the South American continent as sheep having no shepherd, and there was an increasing stream of immigration thither. It is true, that with the exception of British Guiana, England has no territorial possessions in that country; but her sons have gained, and are gradually multiplying, their influence by dint of enterprise and skill, and capital invested there. The spiritual destitution of the British immigrant in Peru, or Chili, or Brazil is not less worthy of attention than in British Guiana, or the Cape of Good Hope; but the favourable consideration of the Church at home is secured for the latter because the British flag waves over them, while the presence of another flag in the former countries has induced the Church to withhold her charities. To correct this state of things has been the aim of the South American Missionary Society. The founder of the Mission, Captain A. Gardiner, was alive to the duty of the Church in this respect, and he bequeathed to the committee of the Society admirable suggestions for meeting the necessities of the case. These suggestions were not without effect; and, during the time that the head-quarters of the Society were at Clifton,* the directors of the work resolved to act upon them as far as possible. In 1861 a resolution to this effect was carried, and the immediate attention of the Rev. A. W. Gardiner to the wants of the British residents at Lota illustrated its force. Out of this grew the missionary chaplaincies of Panama and Callao, funds for the establishment of which were furnished through the liberality of British merchants, whose appreciation of the benefit of the Society's agency had been learned at Lota. In succession, chaplaincies have been established at the Chincha Islands, off the Peruvian coast, at Arica and Tacna in Peru; and on the rivers Uruguay and Plate on the eastern side. And surely it is not too much to hope that wherever English chaplains and English congregations have a local standing in South America, they will desire to extend the knowledge of the gospel to the regions beyond their own

* They were removed to London at the close of the year 1865.

immediate neighbourhood.   We look to them to link their efforts together in a grand effort to preach Christ to the heathens of the interior.   We desire that the gospel may come to them, "not in word only, but also in power and in much assurance," and that from them may be "sounded out the Word of the Lord" in all South America.

PRINTED BY BALLANTYNE, HANSON AND CO.
EDINBURGH AND LONDON